GOTH GIRLS OF BANFF

GOTH GIRLS OF BANFF

stories

JOHN O'NEILL

NEWEST PRESS
EDMONTON, AB

Library and Archives Canada Cataloguing in Publication

Title: Goth girls of Banff : stories / John O'Neill.
Names: O'Neill, John, 1959- author.
Identifiers: Canadiana (print) 20200159976 | Canadiana (ebook) 20200160044 | ISBN 9781988732954
(softcover) | ISBN 9781988732961 (EPUB) | ISBN 9781988732978 (Kindle)
Classification: LCC PS8579.N388 G68 2020 | DDC C813/.54—dc23

NeWest Press wishes to acknowledge that the land on which we operate is Treaty 6 territory and a traditional meeting ground and home for many Indigenous Peoples, including Cree, Saulteaux, Niitsitapi (Blackfoot), Métis, and Nakota Sioux.

Board Editor: Anne Nothof
Cover design & typesetting: Kate Hargreaves
Cover photograph by John Molenaar via Unsplash
Author photograph: Ann Chaban

Canada Council for the Arts Conseil des Arts du Canada

Funded by the Government of Canada Financé par le gouvernement du Canada | Canada

access©

Alberta Government

NeWest Press acknowledges the Canada Council for the Arts, the Alberta Foundation for the Arts, and the Edmonton Arts Council for support of our publishing program. This project is funded in part by the Government of Canada.

201, 8540 – 109 Street
Edmonton, AB T6G 1E6
780.432.9427
www.newestpress.com

No bison were harmed in the making of this book.
PRINTED AND BOUND IN CANADA
2 3 4 5 22 21

For my family
And, as always, for Ann
who sings to keep the bears away

CONTENTS

WHAT IS WRITTEN
or
TALKING TO KEEP THE BEARS AWAY

THE ALLANS PICKED ME UP OUTSIDE CALGARY IN AN OLD Volkswagen van. Gale's arm, with the Road Runner tattoo on it (on the bluish culvert of her wrist, how'd she manage that?) motioned me towards them with, "Long as you don't mind kids."

Long as they don't mind me. The door screeched, slid open, I looked and flinched and stepped up, squeaked along hot vinyl and against two little girls, spokey-legged, knobby-kneed, arms crossed but quick as hummingbirds, arms crossed against me, both with their faces kept straight ahead and both smiling horribly, funnily. Maybe I smelled.

"Do I smell?" I said, sniffing my sweaty pits, exaggerating, and the two girls giggled, the older one less, but still.

Their father—bearded, straggly, barn-door big, hard-necked but soft-eyed—reached a big arm back, shook my hand over his shoulder, hand an unpaved road, said, smiling, "Good for you girls to meet new folks, right? Haven't seen a hitchhiker in weeks. Where you headed?"

"Vancouver, 'ventually. Tough to get a ride. Been four days from Thunder Bay."

"Jeez," said Gale. "People scared of hitchers. Too many horror stories I guess. And then there's that kid attacked on a Greyhound near Winnipeg. Gruesome. Please don't decapitate us. Doesn't seem too much to ask."

She laughed, nearly screamed, voice high and thin like razor barbed wire, caught herself again, put a fist to her mouth, winked at her girls as if to say *I know this ain't too scary for the likes of you.* I caught the bandwagon, said, "I heard stories of hitchhikers getting a lift then meeting *their* makers. Please don't kill me either."

Knew why I'd had such trouble thumbing the flatland, the breadbasket. I was exposed. Folks sensed something, sadness coming off of me like dust, thick and arid, billowing out, telling folks they should leave me well enough alone, like they knew where I was coming from and what I'd done.

Gale screamed, caught herself again, said, "Anyways, Bob here was in the military. He'd snap you like a wishbone." I wondered if Gale was sniffing me out.

Bob said, "You can make a wish."

Gale said, "Don't sweat. He only hurts conservative types and anybody from Ottawa. Left a path of destruction across the east."

The girl nearest me, the older one, stretched her pale arms in front of her, Frankenstein's monster in miniature, said, "Mr. Harper has some good ideas," snapped her bubblegum in exclamation, assassinating the back of the seat.

Her father laughed, "You'll be hitching soon, with that opinion." Caught me in the rearview, said, "Leslie had to follow the election at her school. Was assigned Harper's campaign. Poor girl."

Gale added, out of the quivery blue, "The mountains look like clouds. Hard to believe they're even real."

I looked out, swallowing, but settling in, liking the banter. Tried not to look in the rearview. Shifted so I couldn't. All them yesterdays. Tasted the tang of gasoline and saw, through the cracked windshield, the ridges of mountains between Bob and Gale—there was a fault line in the dirty glass from upper left to lower right, a slash, a lightning strike, the mountains and sky moving below, above it. I tried to remember the Stephen Harper joke that my last ride, a gnarled old woman who wore a purple paisley scarf and whose make-upped face looked like crumbling stucco, had told me, something about "Captain Bloodless, nicknamed the Harpoon and the Sub-Prime Minister." I couldn't. Just the same, I was glad to close my eyes and listen.

The two little girls were bopping and posing and humming, tuned into their iPods. Gale piped up and said, "Girls, unplug. Be sociable." She reached over and tugged their white strings, repeating, "Don't be awful. Talk to the man."

The girls didn't go cold or scowl, just got unwired as required. I scowled for them, said, "Sorry." It was a word I was usin' a lot, strainin' for the straight and narrow.

The small one with the cat glasses and vague unibrow and ears big as her hands didn't miss a beat, said, "Why you hitchhiking? Don't you own a van?"

Her freckled jaw hung open. She was imitating a moron, imitating what she thought of me.

Gale said, "Lee, please."

Before I could laugh or answer or spit, Lee said, "What's your hitchhiker name?"

"Not sure I got one. My name's Don. Don't need a van. Rely on the kindness of strangers." (I thought of telling her my hitchhiker name was Donny Dylan, what they tagged me back in the Bay, after the poet I liked).

The little one slammed her eyes shut, made her best disgusted face, said, "Dawn? That's a girl's name."

Her mom turned again (they oughta make swivel seats in vehicles for people with kids), said, "Lee, it's like your name. Good for girls *and* boys."

The older girl said, "Sorry," torpedoed her sister with an elbow. Lee said, "You can't say sorry for me; it's *my* sorry. I was going to say it, I wanted to hear myself say it, it's my word, isn't it, Mom? Shut up, Leslie *Meslie*." Had to bite my tongue not to say *It's your sorry, don't let anybody take it, that's a dead path.* Lee continued, bouncing in place, "Dad, I have to go pee. I can feel the tide coming, Dad. It's an ocean. You don't want to see the ocean, do you, under these circumstances?"

Their father didn't look around. "We were just … you should have…."

Gale said, "Swimming upstream, Bob, swimming upstream."

"No station till Canmore. I'll pull over if there's a place. You can squat in the bushes. Maybe a bear can wipe your big wet bum-bum."

The little girl laughed, looked bored, bounced big and slapped the roof, said, "Dad, bears don't like bum-bums, specially yours."

She made paper-cut eyes, put them on me. She was wondering how I was with all the pee and bum talk.

Leslie said, "How do you know? Bears eat anything, even skinny, stinky things like you, and they'll probly dip you in honey before they chow down."

Gale said, "Jeez Louise, can we chill? The man's gonna be begging to get out. Sorry, Don. Sure you didn't bargain on being a passenger on the moron bus."

I smiled too stiffly, was out of practice, while Lee rolled her eyes and head, stuck her arms out in front of her as her sister had before. Her arms were as hairy as mine. She started intoning, "We're all morons here; we're all morons here; we're all morons here."

No one reacted. Lee plugged her earphones back in. In a minute, her sister wired up. It was nice. The purr, occasional cough of the engine. Low music thumping from the girls' heads. Ranchland creasing into hills. Wolf sun climbing. Mountains growing closer, white-haired, knuckle-faced. I was wedged in that back seat and the girls had closed their eyes. Jiggly legs shot out from the seat beside me. They both wore the same runners, but the younger one had scribbled on hers, squiggles and faces and arrows and things that looked like donuts, and the words "Girltown" and "Dream." Took me a minute to see these hadn't been drawn on at all, but were part of the design. I imagined Lee picking them out in the store. Imagined her sister's impatience, her sibling, snivelling scorn. Wondered when I might scribble again—hadn't written in weeks, sick unto death of my prison stories, pushing for publication but piling up rejections, wallpaper for the john and paper airplanes for the bowl: "keep writing," "not right for our magazine," "need to develop a stronger voice," and "get a life." I'm out here getting it.

Sank more deeply into the seat. Fought the impulse to pull Lee's earphones free, to stretch the wires against my eyes and nose and mouth, to make a monster face, my face all split into bulgy sections, as if it'd been sewn together. I wanted to groan, to laugh, to go silly in that back seat, to make fun of and try to comb Lee's hairy arms, her little convict arms. I wanted to whine, "Are we almost there? I gotta go pee, I gotta go pee, a tidal wave coming." Back seat of that van was heaven, or some decent imitation. I'd never felt happier. Couldn't believe how easy I was, stuffed up against these girls, these strangers. Couldn't believe how easy they were with me. Back in the Bay, you never got up close with anyone, the smell of another man's flesh meant he was about to shank you or turn you out for a thrill, or ghost you home with a shop wire from ear to ear. You'd crack his skull while the guards looked on. Still had the scar to prove it, pink rosary beads running from right hip to left armpit, and still had bad dreams, rank ones where I didn't see nothing, but felt hot breath like worms in my ear.

Almost happy, what was I lookin' for? Slice of forgiveness, maybe. Thin, dissolving. But no judgment. I'd look judgment square in the eye till it backed off, came back with something better. Course, they couldn't judge me 'cause they didn't know. Better like that.

Bob pulled the van into a circle of dirt by the highway, near a grumbling low ridge of sagebrush and dogwood, said, "This is your chance, Lee. Be careful. Get out on the grass side."

Lee scrambled over her sister, more squeals. Gale also jumped out, shouted after her, "You're not going alone, hold up."

Dad sternly from the window, "Bears. Could be *bears* in there. Make some noise. Keep talking so we know you haven't been eaten."

Found myself thinking that Lee would keep peeing and talking even when sentenced to life inside a bear, like Jonah in the whale.

Lee paused on her way up the hill, put a hand up against her mother's advance, said, "Mom, I can go alone. It's all good."

Gale nodded, turned back, shrugged twice at her husband, it meant, twice, *What can you do*? Lee darted up the slope, parted the bushes with her head, already tugging at her striped shorts.

Leslie, still sitting beside me, said, "Dad, the animals will hear her peein' from a mile away, when girls pee it comes out loud, like, grrrrrr, brrrrrr." She made a sort of liquid avalanche sound, red eyed me as if I couldn't imagine such a thing, like I was born yesterday as one big thumb, like I'd never arrived anywhere. Could feel her scorn, it wasn't for what I'd done but for what I hadn't, *Why's this loser alone, why's this guy without a van or car or skateboard?*

"Shhh, I can't hear," scolded Bob, yelled towards the bushes. "Lee, I can't hear you, I'm not kidding, please talk till you're done."

I looked over and saw that Leslie had closed her eyes, resting in the parole from her sister. I leaned towards the window to hear if Lee followed Dad's orders, heard the little girl's rant. Grinned at the flaming voice coming out of the bush, got serious as though I was Moses listening to sage instructions for something or other. After all, I been doin' a monologue for seven years, talker and hard audience rolled into one.

The brightly burning voice said this: "I don't see the bear tongue guess it doesn't like my bum-bum Leslie told me it'd swallow but Leslie never met the bears she knows wolves did a picture for her school of wolves bigger than horses she used my scissors I'm not supposed to play with and glue and crayons I got for Christmas and made a card of Albert with a bone we both cut Bristol board wolves we picked up a stranger he's funny his name is a girl hit me in the funny bone at school and Ms. Porter said she had to shit sorry sit in the office to see the Principal and Terry said she should get an eternal time out Mom said I should fix my problem and 'pologize to her for seeing the Principal and felt sick like when I ate the sick hotdog at the picnic lake and threw up on Albert the bear won't see me anyway maybe I'll throw up on him or keep talking telling you this story it's a good story so they won't take me where I don't want to go so I'm saying and goin' pee in the dirt I'm an animal from up above funny Dawn's a girl name but he's a boy I guess he's lonely maybe we could sit together in A&W when we go there all the boxes are square but the food is flat are you listening daddy papa-burger are you listening I'm just pulling my pants up and talking to keep the bears away I'm not afraid of bears or dogs or cats with long whiskers they need so they know if they can fit through holes I go through holes I thought there was a hole in my bed and a lady was goin' to come take me away Mom says she's sick and tired but the only girl who'll carry me riding on a dog is hard Albert lets me ride him and licks my face you don't let people lick your face I'm done now I'm all done I kept the bears away but what if the bear got Leslie chewed her dumb bum-bum and Mom and Dad and Dawn in the back seat oh Mom Dad say something I'm fin-ished I'm com-in' out."

Lee came out. Gale slouched and smoked against the passenger side. Bob stayed in his seat but also lit up, neither of them reacting to Lee's monologue. Gale turned and took hold of the door handle, spun her burning cigarette into the dirt, put her grey face close to the window, said, "Awful I know, I'm tryin' to quit, started up again after Lee's birth, she was premature. Was a tough tough year."

Premature. Out too soon. Bawlin' bloody and slight into the world. Bob didn't comment, just kept sucking, pinching the red stub, smoking his cigarette like he had a grudge against it, even when Lee tumbled out of the bushes, tumbled down then up and over me and against Leslie who startled awake and said, "You're, stab-bing, me, stab-bing, me," poking her sister with syllables. Said to her mom, "Let Dad sleep with her tonight, she stabs and farts too much."

Bob flicked his cigarette away, said, "My gas is enough for one bed. One of the pleasures of life is when you fart, trap yourself under the blankets, take a good whiff."

"Dad whatever," Lee said, bending a double-jointed arm like it was broke in front of her sister's face.

"Don't don't don't," Leslie said. "So *gross*. Lee needs a time out."

Gale climbed in, threw a breadloaf arm across the back of the seat, coughed, laughed at something, coughed again (her cough had a weird distance to it, like it was coming from somewhere else, she was a sick ventriloquist) and said to Lee, "I hope you wiped yourself dear."

Lee tightened the laces of her face, said, "I only peed. There's a new river now, goin' to the sea, no worries."

I think about the river she made. Think about *my* time out. Think about Lee's story in the bushes, how she spoke my name. May Brill spoke my name—last thing she did. Think about her gravestone, flat in the earth. Saw it before I quit Kingston, her carved name, close years of birth and death, the words "forever in our hearts." Said a prayer, *Forgive us our trespasses as we forgive*, put both hands on the cold stone, did fifty push-ups there, wished I'd done a thousand that day. Dug my fingernails inside the words, tried to lift it like a trap door, climb inside, stretch out beside her. Didn't know I had anger till she came along. One bad moment stretchin' till now, still stretchin', boneless, like Lee's funny arm. Decided, over her grave, I wouldn't write another story or poem. Maybe I'll write May's story—I'll write her story and put *myself* in it, put myself in it like I'm her sister, mother and dad, no time out from that.

Bob pulled onto the almost bare highway, just a silver Airstream bulleting the other way, catching sunlight, rolling barn fire. Quiet came, post-monologue, post-peepee. There'd been no bear. The mountains had grown. We were shrinking. Sky dead-skin white. Some excitement stirred us when Bob saw a snowy owl on a fencepost—Lee unbuckled, scrambled over me, little fists burning my thighs, just in time to see the owl fly, swoop above the highway's shoulder. Lee scrambled back, stacking elbows and knees, said, "That bird is big as my bed." Gave me a smile, this wide almost-laughing smile, her eyes still seeing the owl, she was showing her still-seeing-the-owl face. My mouth went dry. I almost said *Sorry*. Sorry she was smiling at me, wasting it. I smiled back, felt something crack in my jaw. Leslie, in reply, snorted "No it's *not*," and I said—more rough than I wanted to, all this blackness came up in my throat, scalded my tongue, ate that pink gravestone, went right past the "sorry" there, filled the van so everyone went quiet, Leslie with a scared *What just happened* look—"*YES IT IS*." Even Lee looked at me with her mouth open, as if to say *How would you know, anyways*? Till she smiled at me again.

Bob, glaring in the rearview. He was thinkin' but not sayin' *Don't talk to my daughter that way*. Just fuckin' say it, I thought, just go right ahead. But Lee kept smiling, waitin' and pushin' me to grin, too. So I did, like nothing was wrong. Then, weirdly, nothing was.

Gale twisted around, changed the subject, broke free from the moment, said, "So Vancouver. You got family there, or is this a solitary adventure?"

"Solitary," I said. "Came out here after high school. Wanted to see it again."

"Perfect," Bob said. "No one to answer to. Was out here when I was in school, worked two summers at the Banff

Springs. Wanted to show the girls where Daddy scrubbed dishes, went rock climbing along the Bow."

Silence now, Gale open towards me, knowing a wounded thing, and Bob watchin' in the rearview, both waiting on the edge of me telling them more. Why was this forty-something-year-old hitchhiking alone? What was he leaving? A question mark hovered in the air, was the crooked shape of the gap of the mountains before us. Bookend mountains. They wanted to include me in their story, wanted to hear my history to know where, or if, it collided with theirs.

But I held my mud—it was no time to tell them I was runnin', no time to tell them I'd done time. Was sure the right moment would come. Maybe a few sentences spoke by some gas pumps, while the girls ate licorice, punched through magazines. I felt I owed them. I still needed to earn my place in that back seat, especially after sharing Lee's story, like a dream overheard, or a promise, or a childish confession whose innocence includes the listener but never betrays you. Could feel forgiveness coming, sure as the mountains, sure as the sky was shrinkin' back. But not forgiveness *spoken*—it was just *being*, the idea of being, the idea of calm, of peace, starting with this family, the idea that the world might, *Fuck the world,* allow me in again.

This is all I remember. Try to recall the exact details, the sequence of events, but can't, sure only that, had I not been there, tucked in beside Leslie and Lee, it probably wouldn't have happened. I changed things, threw things out of whack. One thought gave birth to another. One word led to another, a pause, a backward glance, action, reaction, stream of events, like Lee's monologue in the bushes, her peepee story. Life like that, a jumble of things, details that, after the event, seem to lead inexorably to it, dumb to tell. Maybe this is what killed them, nature calling, then nature calling again, like a bear attack. And had Lee's story been quicker, or slower, more careful in the telling. Or if they hadn't stopped to give a stranger a ride, or if Bob hadn't been, after my flare-up, readin' me in the rearview.

I'd dozed off, Lee curled tight beside me, woke when we'd entered the corridor of mountains, knife-blade peaks at my side. Something shifted against them, like the shadow of clouds, or a mudslide, or curtain of animals sweeping across stone. I thought without thinking of Leslie and Lee, I wanted to share and blurted out, louder than I needed to, and at exactly the same time that Lee spoke, was suddenly squirming against her seatbelt, I don't know what she said because I was saying, "Look girls, something is moving on the mountain."

At that precise moment, the investigating officer explained, a semi coming in the other direction hit an elk, sent it spinning into our lane—antlers like uprooted and drifting trees, avalanche of bone and flesh and fur—crashed full on into our windshield. I still remember hooves screeching the hood, and hair, and thin white arms like whips, nothing else.

Bob lost control. Lost everything. We spun, flipped, slid across the asphalt where the same truck that had launched the animal hit us, dragged us under. I wasn't there. Their bodies were taken back to Calgary and I went too—bruised, concussed, black-eyed yet seeing clearly, begging a zippered bag for myself. When we'd spun I'd been thrown clear, landed in bushes that broke my fall, simple, terrible as that.

They were the Allans I found out later, more than Gale, Bob, Leslie, Lee.

I went back there and left some flowers, a little stuffed button-eyed bear for Lee, for Leslie, for their mom and dad, memorial by the roadside. Found, halfway up the hill, their wrecked rearview, fragment of metal and glass, thought of tiltin' it against me, pulling it cross both my arms. Instead, in dumb commemoration, peed in that broken place. Stayed at the Motel 6 on Mission Street, watched, from my window, the mountains growing colder, my hands against the glass, my sentence done, my sentence just beginning, swallowed whole by the event, as if I didn't have enough to forgive, forget, with nothing to forgive, the mountains held against my throat with a truck's grille, animal's antlers, a mother's laugh and six-year-old girl, talking to keep the bears away.

And, oh yes, it was words I saw falling, cascading from the ridge, sweeping down and across like a mortal sign. Words on a gravestone, words sheared off its face, words that damage and preserve, a prison story, story you don't know, this family won't ever know, you provide it. Or, better, Lee's monologue in the bushes. Was it her monologue or mine? Family stopped to pick me up: family stopped to let her talk. Which is it? I'm not talking. No seatbelt to confine me, no walls or men's eyes, but strapped forever into recall. I'll talk about it or not talk about it. Write about it or won't write about it. I'll go down believing or not believing, it is written.

ATHABASCA

A FRIEND AT WORK WHO SHARED HER PINCHED LIFE OF chronic pain had suggested the trip out west, knowing that Karen had a sister there. She also knew the relationship between them was, as she said gleefully, *Fraught*. She pushed Karen anyway, openly anticipating all of the horror stories that might return with her friend like cheap but colourful souvenirs. "Glacier-fed lakes, wild creatures, omnivorous sister," Pearl teased as they sat in the Tim Hortons near the school—sisters by virtue of hurt—before cataloguing, as they routinely did, what they'd each be willing to give up if the exquisite pain would disappear from their lives, a coffee-and-cruller deal with God. Karen couldn't remember who sacrificed what on the list they'd compiled since first discovering that they were both living with the same affliction that pinpointed the brain as the acoustic location of their torment:

"I'd trade ten years of my life."

"I'd be willing not to have kids."

"I'd be willing to have kids."

"I'd go blind in one eye."

"Deaf in one ear."

"A horrible death."

"I'd accept *your* horrible death."

"I'd go to church three times a week."

"Once a month."

"To never have sex again."

"Wouldn't be much of a change for *me*."

The two women always ended up in raucous laughter, honking at the ceiling, making whirlpools in their lattes, investing as much as they could in the moments when migraine didn't visit, like their surly co-worker Elton (Karen refused to call him *colleague*), who often showed up at their coffee hole but never felt constrained to come over and knee-slap with the two barking ladies.

Karen had come west, was lifting her head to the window of her sister's SUV, pressed her grieving eye to the glass. They drove through the prairie storm, neurons firing and synapses blazing in the aching skull of the sky, but she'd have to *Hang on, hang on, girl* (she imagined Pearl there, curled and miraculous and nodding towards her, stroking the back of her neck) till she could retrieve her medication.

"Better than Ontario storms," her sister Sylvie said, hands on the wheel, muscles in her arms flexing and streaked with wet shadows. "Can see it coming for miles," she explained, waving an arm along the dashboard, as if Karen could see beyond their storm-pummelled, wind-pummelling hood.

"Why the fuck we in the *middle* of it then?" Karen asked, hands between her knees. She was trying not to throttle her own face.

"No worries," Sylvie said. "Nearly out of it. Ten years, haven't been struck yet."

It wasn't the storm anyway. Not the rain sliding in collapsing tables off the highway, not the semis dropping windows of water to shatter on their hood. It wasn't even the smug wiry thinness of Sylvie's husband Ron, who, after crushing the bones in her hand, said, "So, you've finally come to Canada's beatin' heart." (She'd arrived the night before, and he had arced his elbow up because he wanted her to notice, and she did, the sinewy, sun-baked, drained-ditch toughness of his prairie forearm, and the Rolex on his wrist, big as a baby's face). It wasn't even their soaring house on the edge of Drumheller, the guest room so vast she kept waking in the crying coyote night, afraid some animal was skulking in its hidden alcoves with a hungry hate on for Toronto. It was none of these things, really—it was the prodromal migraine stage that now seemed more of an injustice, thrown into relief by the badlands. But, okay, down to greening brass tacks, it was her sister's *attitude* that was the worst aspect of migraine—whenever Karen mentioned her illness, Sylvie got this look, dark and dour, equal parts pity and skepticism (never mind that Sylvie surely got this look from long nights wondering if Ron really was coming home late because yet another granite countertop installation, in the McMansion of another oil-drenched exec, had taken longer than scheduled). Though Sylvie knew that her sister was taking time off because of her condition, she still carried herself around their fat hoodoo house as if Karen were plain crazy—but not *plain* crazy, not *prairie farmland nerve-ends blowing like tumbleweeds under too much open sky* crazy, but *Toronto, privileged, skyscraper glass treadmill centre-of-the-universe* crazy, where pain was as garish, thin and fake as a plastic repro of the CN Tower.

Yet Karen wondered, cowering in the SUV, if her foul moods were a consequence of her illness, or whether they were a part of her personality—she remembered a sunnier girl, but, increasingly, that girl seemed to be someone else, like a dimly recalled childhood friend. Perhaps if migraine was removed from her life, she'd still look at the world as if one half of it was always shrouded, as if one half of it always throbbed. She would *try, try, try* on this trip, to prevent the anticipation of pain from spoiling her mood.

Now, sunlight was bouncing up hard from the highway. Karen watched the downtown towers of Calgary rise up, too. Felt as though she were looking at something tainted. Pearl had advised her, imitating the gait and twang of an inebriated gunslinger, hand on holster and itchin' to draw, "Skip Calgary, it's a two-bit, cowboy-dumb, wild west town; dirty and low-down and leaves the tang of horse piss in your mouth, no matter how 'phisticated it tries to be." Though Pearl had only been to Calgary once, for an education conference where she *did* get inebriated, roaring drunk—it was only a week after her divorce was finalized—and missed all of the workshops on the first two of the three days, Karen still added this to her bartering list, "I'll skip every Canadian city, except for Edmonton, Vancouver, St. John's, and of course Montreal."

West of the city they stopped for gas. Sylvie had sped by several self-serve stations, preferring, she said, "The luxury of the full-serve with its erotic connotations." But Karen had explained to Sylvie that she needed, *Pronto*, to take her medication or that her prodromal state would launch into an aura, the point of no return, but that her pills were locked in the trunk. In the rush of their preparations—Sylvie couldn't get away from Ron fast enough—she'd stashed them into a sleeve of her suitcase.

"Of course," Sylvie said, "But it'll only be another minute to a full-serve, then we both get what we want."

What did her sister want, anyway? Karen never understood. And she couldn't, okay *could* believe that her sister was ignoring her, insisting on directing things, as she had done since they were girls, negotiating for scuffed, naked Barbies on the floor of their bedroom, a thousand years and ten thousand arguments ago. When Sylvie finally swung the SUV under the Shell sign, Karen didn't wait for the vehicle to come to a full stop, but opened the door and jumped running onto the pavement, while her sister popped the trunk and laughed a little, probably because Karen, wild and blurry and annoyed, looked like a bad CGI effect, *Jurassic* sister.

Once she'd wrestled her pills free, Karen strode between gas pumps and into the convenience mart, ignoring the stares of the men who were dragging dripping squeegees across dragonflies, bats, tail feathers, and insects fused to windshields and grilles. Felt a twinge of pleasure in their occupations, how satisfying it would be to scrape and wash away death so easily. This feeling vanished as she paused before the glass cooler doors and stared, overwhelmed, at the rows of water bottles, all the brands, the wasteful extravagance of mere bottled water pretending to be sweet elixirs. Thought of Sylvie and Ron's top-of-the-line refrigerator, a tall black monolith like the one from *2001*, how it made its own ice, and had a freezer that, like a glacier, could preserve a whole Mastodon. Karen thought how nice that might be—to crawl into a glacier and let ice take over, let ice do its icy work. To preserve oneself, to wake up later when they'd have a cure for migraine, when medical science had caught up to her despair.

Karen cracked open the bottle's plastic cap and took a long sucking swig and, throwing her head back, popped the tablet.

Back outside, she almost ran into Sylvie behind the wall of gas pumps. Her sister was leaning against the SUV, chatting up the attendant, a young man in yellow coveralls and with a windburnt, brick-coloured face, and with the same sinewy and tanned arms as Ron. He leaned against the gas funnel, his hip cocked towards Sylvie, offering a giddy-up saddle she could squeeze between her too thin, blue-jeaned, cowgirl thighs.

Karen glanced down, saw that some of the water she'd guzzled had drizzled onto her top, leaving a swath of wetness across her chest. Her nipples protruded obscenely. It was an unscheduled wet T-shirt contest, and she was the leading contestant. This sort of thing was probably common in Calgary, wet T-shirt contests as routine as tack stores and chinooks. Before she could escape and giggle to herself, before she could happily collapse and concentrate on the Maxalt RPD going to work in her stomach, her sister laughed and said to the attendant, "This is my sis, Karen, I was telling you about. Works with kids and wants one, but she's from *Toronto*."

Karen froze. The young man, eyes on her face and his free hand hooked inside a belt loop, said, "Sorry I can't shake your hand miss, got oil on everything. I hear you're visiting. Be honoured to show you round. Don't do this sort of thing, but your sister said. Ah. Never mind. I mean, it's all right. These things sure eat up gas, don't they?"

He'd sensed her mortification. Or he'd glanced down and her nipples weren't to his liking, too long, too sad and downturned, like the nozzle on the gas pump. She grunted "uh-huh," walked around and got inside the vehicle. Could hear a muffled exchange between her sister and the man, something about a horrendous crash that occurred on the Trans-Canada recently, a whole family killed. Sylvie climbed in, stabbed the ignition. They fishtailed onto the highway. Sylvie didn't speak, and she seemed relaxed, but this laxness was betrayed by her expression—mouth tight, enduring, the fullness of her lips sucked inside. Sylvie was, *Looks good on her*, eating her own face.

Soon, they turned off the main highway in Canmore and onto a parallel gravel road, then onto a dirt road that led to the cabin they'd reserved, one of a dozen that encircled a dirty campfire pit and faced, on the other side of the highway, the Three Sisters, a trio of jagged peaks that loomed over the town. Sylvie's mouth hardened again when she saw how dilapidated the cabins were—the eaves hanging loose, the porches peeling dry in the sun, wedges of green flaking up from the wood, also protruding rusty nails, big as railway spikes.

Sort of beautiful, Karen thought. Sylvie said, "I thought, *shit*, these were the same cabins Ron and I stayed in last summer. These are awful. We'll find another place."

"It's okay, they're rustic. I need a break from the road."

"This irritates me. Let me find another place."

"Sylvie."

"We'll check out the town. I'll handle it."

"Sylvie, *I need to have a break*."

"Sorry, whatever," Sylvie said, simultaneously screeching the SUV into one of the parking spaces below the wrecked cabins.

So this was it, Karen thought—same old theme running through this vacation—Karen the afflicted, complaining one, and Sylvie the strong, take-control, semi-happily married one. Nothing new, even in this mountain place.

Karen tensed up further when she saw three teenagers lounging or decomposing on the porch of one of the cabins, sitting on a bench jammed close, wires trailing from their ears. Their iPhones kept them separate yet together, in the kind of mindless but occupied state that Karen recognized. She was back in her Toronto classroom where she was coaxing words from Laverne, one of her special-needs kids, a girl who, it took them weeks to discover, had to start every one of her sentences with her middle name, "Felice," before she could write anything else. And who insisted on sitting beside Reed, a happy burly boy with a face like chewed bubblegum, who punctuated each of his scribbled sentences by spitting on the floor (the Resource room was a veritable Jacuzzi of bodily fluids), a kind of involuntary physical manifestation of what he'd expectorated in ink onto his paper. Karen had placed a plastic bucket beneath his desk, believing they should accommodate this peculiarity until it could be further explored. But she got into a nasty argument with Elton Creel, who insisted that the kids exploited her. Karen told him, unwilling to debate the matter (Elton loved to debate, ironic spittle bubbling on his own lips) in a seething low voice, "They've got enough fucking problems. Let them exploit us a little." All this came back to her, not so much the challenges of working with the students, but the strain of trying to reconcile her own views with those of her co-workers. Except of course for Pearl—she and Pearl were always on the same ragged but beautiful page.

Karen and Sylvie managed to settle into something resembling tranquility in their matching, dilapidated Muskoka chairs. Late that afternoon, Sylvie had borrowed a hammer from the teenage desk clerk and pounded the protruding porch nails out of harm's way. While Sylvie examined her purplish toenails in the failing mountain light, Karen studied the alpenglow on the peaks opposite them.

For the first time since Sylvie had steered the SUV with its gritted-teeth grin out of their three-car garage, not acknowledging Ron as he waved goodbye, good riddance, between the pillars of their house, Karen understood why somebody might pull up roots and journey west. She stared at the peaks and felt a strange stirring. It wasn't sexual. But she felt like it almost was, or should have been. The alpenglow highlighted a set of crevices, a scarf of fresh snow. She imagined herself curling inside a cave there, embracing some column of stone till her chronic pain flowed into it. She felt easy, and when she looked down, was surprised to find the bulbs of her knobby knees still pushing up through her tights and her little loaf of belly rising from under her T-shirt.

Sylvie, as if sensing the mix of longing and contentment in her sister, as if this were disagreeable, said, "You know, Karen, I was only trying to help. I know you're lonely. You've got to make an effort sometimes, if you want change."

"Sylvie I'm not lonely, I'm *ill*."

"But where does your illness come from? It *means* something."

The snow under the alpenglow melted away. Just a grimace of rock now, a pair of cracked dry lips, *Elton's* cracked dry lips. Karen imagined them grating her neck like a carrot. She said, "That's crap, Sylvie. You know where my illness comes from? Mother had migraines. Her mother had migraines. I don't need to meet someone. That doesn't solve things. *Men* don't solve things. You more than anyone should know that."

Sylvie ignored this, said, "But you told me your migraines got worse after Aubrey left. Didn't you say sadness adds to chronic pain? What, am I losing my mind?"

"Aubrey didn't leave. And I said they got bad right *before* Aubrey left. Before I *kicked him out*. Yeah, loneliness can be a problem, but it's not about me. Sylvie, you don't listen. And one of the things that adds stress is people giving advice."

Sylvie had given advice about Aubrey too, but Karen should have known, with a guy named Aubrey. At first, she'd loved his name, but he lived up, or down, to it—dark, quiet, poetic (he talked about her migraine affliction in edifying, poetic terms) became morose, silent, unemployable. She had loved him, sort of. A little bit. She hated her sister. All the mountains in the world, their remote beauty, couldn't compensate.

"Right," Sylvie said. "I'm sorry. I just thought. Forget it. I'll make some tea. Would you like some tea?"

When Sylvie returned from the cabin with two flowery cups tinkling in their saucers, Karen had a large square of cardboard spread on her lap and across the arms of her Muskoka chair.

"Got this from my bag," she said. "Thought you might like to see it. A collage I made in our chronic pain group."

Sylvie set the teacups down and pulled her chair close. On a creased piece of Bristol board was a vortex of images, whirling towards the centre: pictures of a brain-shaped asteroid, a dump truck, and an ominous black skyscraper with a crack down the middle. Pictures, too, of more personal things: a bottle of pills, a man's brogue shoe, and what looked like a makeup bag, spilling its contents. These fragmented images, though small in real life, were larger than the cut-outs of the asteroid and truck and skyscraper. They were placed closer to the centre where a human figure lay curled up. Also, while the rest of the images had been cut from magazines, the human figure had been sketched in ink, head towards the bottom of the page. From its head another line of ink became a dollar sign, upon which was glued the tiny image of a racehorse.

Sylvie pointed at this, laughed and said, "That's gotta represent Dad."

Karen laughed. "Also the idea of having to win."

Sylvie relaxed back into her seat. "I blame Dad for everything," she said. "Now we want men who are never there."

"We find that focusing on these images, these stress points, diminishes them."

"Positive visualization."

"I'm trying," said Karen with finality, but also with sarcasm, referring not to the collage, or to her chronic pain group, but to the present circumstances.

Sylvie said, "That's all anyone can expect."

Karen said, "And who do you mean by *anyone*?"

She said this, too, with edge, and immediately regretted it—after all, her sister was being sympathetic, hadn't dismissed her collage as juvenile or an exercise in self-pity. Sylvie *was* trying. The tingle at the back of Karen's neck, this time, was disappointment in herself, and another not-so-distant-early-warning. Her migraine threatened again.

THE NEXT MORNING, THEY DROVE TO LAKE LOUISE. The temperature dropped as they moved up the steep mountain road, past the small, cottage-like lodges that lined the way, until they arrived at the crowded parking lot behind the ultimate wilderness cabin, the flat-faced stone *Fairmont Chateau Lake Louise*. The lake was beautiful, Karen had to admit, though she found herself resisting the beauty, focusing instead on the crowds of tourists on its edge, all of them milling around, posing, talking, and holding their iPhones over their heads, taking selfies, or trying for unobstructed views of the lake and the symmetrical mountains that framed it.

There was a kind of nervousness, a frantic sense of event that threatened the landscape's tranquility. "Too many humans ruin beauty," Karen thought. Her idea was illustrated when Sylvie pulled out a magazine photo of Lake Louise and held it up, as if this legitimized their experience. Her sister was adding to her chronic pain collage. Karen said, "Yeah, I can see the real thing, Sylvie," but wondered whether the real thing really mattered? Karen knew that her sister was happy to be introducing her to this place, but this is precisely what annoyed her. Sylvie kept referring to the sculptured grounds and turquoise lake and shining glaciers as if she owned them, had some special claim to their mystery, including the Chateau in her catalogue, calling it "one of our historic twins," though Karen's first impression was of a prison, with its formidable towers and its windows in straight, unyielding rows.

While the sisters sat before their expensive salads at the Chateau restaurant, Karen imagined the new collage she'd create based on this vacation: the fat columns on the porch of her sister's Drumheller house; her sister's black driving gloves; a windshield squeegee whose ribbed handle metamorphosed into a cowboy's penis; Ron's sinewy arms—no, strike that, *nothing* about Ron—and her sister's tight mouth and condescending silences. But how to represent such silences that were invariably followed by Sylvie's hushed suggestions on how Karen might better deal with her excruciating, world-twisting pain?

THE ICEFIELDS PARKWAY ROSE AND FELL BETWEEN THE mountains, last leg of the first half of their journey. At the bitter end of it—Karen and her sister mostly silent for the three-plus hours—they descended from a hair-raising climb and reached the Columbia Icefield. Parked at the Visitor Centre. Karen couldn't look at the wide plain across from the building, the Athabasca Glacier creeping like a dead bloodless tongue towards the highway. Even a peripheral glimpse of it made her shiver. It was too monstrous, too cold. Karen needed an intimate, temperate environment. Calming, comforting. As she put on her puffy white jacket, and placed a hand over her eyes, trying to fend off the icy light, her sister spread her arms and let out a happy screech, ready to embrace the frigid air.

When they'd first approached the toe of the glacier, Karen mentioned that she'd heard that glaciers were shrinking because of what scientists believed was global warming. But Sylvie argued this was just a natural phase, the earth just doing what it does. *No way is this man-made,* she barked, though

Karen hadn't said anything about causes. This annoyed Karen, she almost said, *What the fuck do you know about it, wake up and smell the burning coffee.* But she also knew that Ron got much of his kitchen reno work from folks who worked in the oil industry. She could feel the presence of her migraine, like a bear outside a tent, but it had not entered, not yet. Perhaps, if she could rest, things would be all right.

The Visitor Centre offered no reprieve: it was crowded with tourists, with loud children freed from back seats, with adults rummaging for souvenirs that reduced the mountains to portable parodies. People flooded the gift shop, relieved to be able to take a snow globe in hand, to cuddle a plush grizzly bear. Karen kept her eyes on her black running shoes, looked up once to see that Sylvie had joined the line at the Information desk, above which was a huge map of the Icefield. Its blue and red topographical lines reminded Karen of the MRI image of her brain she had pinned up in the closet of her Toronto bedroom.

Karen wandered into the Natural History section. Here, there was some relief. It seemed that folks weren't interested in history, natural or otherwise. She stopped to examine a tree fragment in a glass display case. A little card explained that it was some 8,000 years old, from a tree that had been felled by the frozen river when this valley was being carved by glaciers. It also resembled a hand, the leathery fist of a corpse, like the photograph of a Danish bog person she'd seen once. Karen ignored the warning and leaned on the glass, pictured a tree spread out against advancing ice, imagined the trunk groaning, snapping, and the length of it falling. She felt pleasure in this, how surrender might be a sort of mastery. Maybe, if her migraine took over, she'd become something else, something better. So this was the point of the Mindfulness Meditation she'd been practicing. Pearl always advised her, *Focus on the pain till its contours change.* With these thoughts, one shape leading to another, the fallen tree like a tree of thought, each fibrous branch sprouting a new idea—Karen felt the tingle of wickedness in her, delight in the notion of surrender. Sylvie was suddenly behind her, poking her. Karen started, stepped away.

"What is it?" Karen said. "Why are you lurking?"

"I hope this is okay. I hope you don't get mad. I'm not lurking."

"Mad at what?"

"Got us tickets for the glacier tour. They take you where you can't walk. If you don't want to, I can sell them. It'd be nice to be, you know, to let someone else…."

Sylvie's words were pushing, pushing. Karen felt them against her eardrum. She put up her hand. "No, it's fine. It'll be nice, you're right." Karen turned, gave a last look at the knot of tree, followed her sister to the tour waiting area.

After a delay resulting from a small boy spilling half his ketchup-splattered French fries into his mother's lap, to which she hardly reacted, just produced a wet napkin and cleaned herself, then wiped her son's face with hard little jabs, they were all led outside to the glacier snow coach. It was a huge, bulbous, insect-like cab riding on top of a dozen rubber tires. They found themselves squeezed into small seats among mostly well-padded tourists. Whiffs of strong sweet perfume. Once the driver had inserted earplugs and manoeuvred the vehicle down an embankment and beneath the main highway, the tour guide, a grinning, uniformed young man, began to shout information about the glacier's history, but prefaced his happy harangue with the promise that they would play some "games" later on. *Oh sweet fuck,* Karen thought. *Please leave us alone, you've no idea, we've got enough games going on.*

The tour guide had a handsome face, carved and hard, but it was a face undermined: he had stupid eyes that were too big and enthusiastic, and a long wedge of blond bang like a soft horn. He kept leaning over the front seats, making the woman who sat there press into the man next to her. After the guide shared some facts about the glacier's features, he whispered a grim anecdote, warning them about the dangers of the ice: "Last summer, a mother and her teenage son, ignoring the rules, went beyond the rope barrier. He fell into a shallow crevice, but was so wedged in it took the rescue team three hours to get him out. Eventually, he died, not from hypothermia, but a concussion. Cerebral *he-ma-to-ma*. Shouldn't tell you, but his poor momma got a bill from Parks Canada for the rescue costs. So, please folks, when we leave the snow coach, don't go beyond the rope."

He shared the story with a cloying, self-important sadness that made Karen want to slap him. But she decided this was preferable to his manic enthusiasm, how he segued, without pause, into one of the games he'd mentioned earlier: he got all of the passengers to introduce themselves to the persons sitting immediately around them, but by using their second names, followed by the name of whatever street they lived on. Sylvie became *Jane Coyote Place*. Karen became *Ann St. Clair*. Karen wished her second name was some variation of *Eat Shit And Die*. When the guide announced that actors in the adult film industry often chose their names this way, there were shrieks of laughter, a sort of excited shock at the slightly risqué humour.

Karen noticed that one old couple (he with finely trimmed sideburns and a little tweed cap, she with boyishly cut white hair) had an air of refinement about them, the way they were both sitting perfectly upright and the way she turned her whole body towards him when they spoke—and they didn't laugh at the guide's jokes. She loved the two of them. Unfortunately, the young man saw this, and their lack of rote enthusiasm became his target. Once he'd explained the rules of the campfire "sing-song," he assigned the old couple the first chorus part. When the song began, they sang their part with gusto. Karen stopped loving them. She sank into her seat, lifting her knees, pressing her knuckles into her eye sockets, *counter pressure*, though her migraine hadn't entirely taken hold. The tour guide noticed and yelled over the singing, "We've lost someone, let's sing till she joins in." Karen managed to lift her head—she was the eye of this storm of idiocy—and joined in, though she just mouthed the words. Her face became contorted, her right eye closed, her left rolling back. She looked demented. The tour guide, disturbed, brought the song to an end. The snow coach, on cue, circled and stopped. They had arrived. So had her migraine. Too many changes, not in the barometric pressure, but in the behaviours she was obliged to display. Darkness washed over her, and a terrible spinal throb that felt as though it began at the earth's core. It was a rumbling, an earthquake, a pulverizing tour of pain that Karen alone experienced.

Sylvie, recognizing the problem, said, too little, too late, "I'm sorry, sorry, for dragging you out here. Can I do anything? You want to stay here? I'll stay with you."

"No, I'm." She didn't want to, wanted to, couldn't talk. "A little walk can't hurt."

Tears streamed down her face. Sylvie used the sleeve of her red fleece jacket to wipe them away, then guided Karen out of the coach. Outside, Karen recoiled from her sister, as if the migraine were flowing through her arm, as if Sylvie extended and worsened the pain.

Karen said to her, loudly, crazily, "Really, I'll be okay. Appreciate if you'd give me space."

Sylvie stepped clear, pulled out her iPhone. Moved towards the other passengers who were drifting along the perimeter of the roped-in area. Karen, trying to lift her eyes above the wall of her migraine, struck out alone.

She moved around the snow coach towards a lightning strike of glacier that fell from a black cloud of rock on the far side of the valley. She opened her mouth, tried to relax her face, as if it were a small animal that might pull free of her condition. Then she saw, before her, the yellow rope. Stepped over it. *Embrace the pain, let it be, you will change.* Felt some ease until she heard shouting. She looked back to see the tour guide gesturing, not at her, but at Sylvie, who'd also gone beyond the rope barrier. Both of them were bad, bad girls. All the other tourists were leaning towards Sylvie. No one noticed Karen, as she was hidden somewhat by the snow coach. Inside it, the driver had a newspaper open in his lap, but he was asleep.

Karen walked on. The ice was crosshatched and brittle, dirty too, but just ahead was a fresh powdering of snow. Occasionally, in the prickly net that crunched under her feet was a bright sliver, like a light in the window of a snow-covered house. She crouched near one of these. It was a hole, little corkscrew of blue. How far did it penetrate? When did it cease? What purpose did it serve, this hole in things, this beautiful flaw in the pattern? Karen was reminded of how, she'd read it somewhere, weavers who worked on medieval tapestries often included a flaw, with the idea that nothing should ever be absolutely perfect. Jesus, she thought, why would anyone want to *impose* imperfection?

She noticed a branch, half embedded in ice. It was long but desiccated, like the tree fragment she'd studied in the Visitor Centre. Maybe this was its mother: it had the same consistency, the same yellowish-black hue, and it was trapped in the same ice. She thought of her father's hands when he was near death, bunched up and grey, like old dishcloths. Felt a wave of resentment, surmising that the rope barrier wasn't meant to keep tourists safe, but to prevent them from exploring the past.

She wanted to touch the branch. It was shaped by ice, curved down and out of sight. It was a rope connected to something, like a pull cord between mountains. She would know some relief, she was sure, if she gripped that stick, yanked hard on it. This was a technique a former doctor had suggested: focus your attention on something outside yourself, allow your pain to gather there. It was like the impulse she'd felt back in the Visitor Centre, when the boy had spilled his fries—she wanted the mother to take the boy and shake him. The woman's patience irritated her. Sometimes, Karen thought, men need a good shake. The world needs a good shake. Her sister needed a good shake. Her migraine throbbed in anticipation: she could feel it in her fingernails, in her teeth, in her earlobes, her eyelashes. She stepped towards the branch and over the glacier's little eye of blue. The eye blinked and the ice gave way.

Karen saw the gas station's attendant's hard handsome face; the three teenagers on their porch bench; her sister's husband's forearms; a bolt of lightning jumping from prairie sky to earth. She wasn't seeing her whole life flash before her eyes—only a few meagre images, some of the last ones. This was unfair. She tried, as she fell, to increase herself, thrust her elbows out, pressed her heels against the rushing wall of ice. Why didn't her migraine arrest her fall? Why didn't it sprout dark wings? Wasn't it good for anything?

She came to rest on an ice ledge. Knees against her chest. Right arm crushed in darkness. Her head lolled forward then back, met a frozen pillow. Instantly, images of the other tourists—the old couple holding hands, her sister striding away from her, the suddenly wan face of the tour guide—all seemed a distant memory, as if she'd fallen into a fissure of time as well as space.

Embarrassed by her predicament, she thought of this vast frozen ocean, decided she wouldn't panic, but the fear arrived in gusts: she was breathing too hard, the ice would melt around her, she'd slip farther down, drown. She had to be calm, *Calm*. She shouted the word calm, repeated it, whispered it and pretended it was Pearl speaking, imagined Pearl's warm hand on her neck, the gentle rub, Pearl laughing, *Hey bitch, what you doin' in that ice cube?* Tried to focus on a lesson from her chronic pain group, what was it again? To visualize the source of, ah, the pain, or not the pain but the. . . .

She couldn't remember.

Couldn't see much. Only, ahead of her, a faint blue glow, where another fissure admitted sunlight. She reached up and touched her face, realized she'd lost her sunglasses in the fall. No, she'd lost them on the plane. No, she'd left them in Toronto. No, she didn't know. After a few moments, her eyes adjusting, the glow intensified into a bright arc. The arc contained a shape. Human shape. Karen put her free hand above her eyes and inclined forward, like a sailor searching the horizon. Bit her lip hard at what she saw there.

The arc of blue held a woman's body, an ample one, but upside down. Karen closed her eyes, waited. Tried to blink the image away. The woman was still there, not more than fifteen feet in front of her, draped in dark fabric that bunched around broad shoulders, and with black hair that hung in frozen ropes. Her feet, in short lace-up boots, were crossed at the ankles, and protruded from a skirt that resembled a dark bell, toes pointed daintily towards the sky. One of her arms angled out from her side, and she gripped something, maybe a walking stick. She appeared to be from the early twentieth century, maybe older. Karen wasn't sure. But what *was* certain—she hadn't been rescued. Perhaps she was that rare thing, an early female explorer who had rejected the world and struck out alone, went missing. Or, like those Danish bog people, she'd been the victim of some ancient ritual sacrifice. What contradicted this impression, though, was one detail—the woman's inverted face was indistinct, blurred by ice, a hand resting on her cheek. This created the sense she was at ease, was patiently waiting. Karen's breathing slowed and she felt, staring at the figure, a sense of privilege. She wasn't sure what to do with this feeling. And she noticed, beyond the woman, where sunlight penetrated, other fissures. She imagined that each of them contained a female body, that the glacier was rife with female humanity, bodies suspended, preserved, forgotten. It also occurred to Karen that most of the tourists who'd gone on the glacier tour, with only three exceptions, were women. What were they searching for out on this cold, unforgiving immemorial plateau, wedged between mountains?

In the clarity of her contemplation, its intensity, there was no room for fear. Her migraine's passing had left an empty space, which she didn't want to fill. It, too, was substantial. But the migraine was more than gone—Karen had the sense that its cruel aura, if she survived, would never visit her again. Despite her cramped position, she was airy, weightless. An impression came to her, a sick memory, of all the medications she'd been taking, the mountains of pills prescribed over the years by a perpetual parade of doctors, most of them men. She needed to experience something different. Something ineffable, eternal, needed to take her in, even though, even now, she didn't want to give it a name. But she knew it was female. The glacier was female. But she *would* give it a name—Sylvie. Why not? Her sister was alone, too. Substantially alone. Her sister had brought her here, and she was grateful. Sort of grateful. As she stared at the blue light and that woman's body in front of her, she lightened and lightened, a breeze playing through her pain-free skull. She was convinced, if she just waited long enough, she'd float free.

She hardly noticed when a rope, heavy, rough, yellow, looped at the end, struck her head and fell by her free arm. It was an inconvenience. She didn't know how much time had passed. Wasn't sure if she was numb, delirious, dead, or happy. She'd have to decide. She wasn't sure what to do. She'd have to think about it longer. But that was easy. Her head was clear.

ATTACKING THE BEAR

OKAY, YEAH, I KNOW WHAT THE BROCHURE SAYS: "BACK away slowly. Make yourself big by lifting your arms. Drop your backpack, distract the animal. Or take a rock and have done with it; bludgeon yourself to death, 'cause the bear will do worse." So my first impulse is dead wrong—I don't do what's required. Instead, I slip my hand into the pocket of my green fleece jacket and pluck out my black sketchbook, a number 4 pencil tucked into the spine. And with the book in my hands, and the bear swinging its head forth and back, like the trailer on a careening semi, or an angry, eye-popping dad who you long to put your arms around but can't, I freeze. The sketchbook feels heavy as a door. Will it be any use in fighting off a bear? What will a book do to a big surly animal?

But I'm *not* frozen by fear, let's be straight. And the bear, scary as he is, clearly hasn't made up his mind—he's sideways to me, hulky profile backlit by sun, set against what looks like a divider of autumn leaves, a kind of glowing Chinese screen, like the one beside my massage table at the spa where I work. Also, he looks like a sofa, one of those old ones with all the bulky curves and wanking wood trim. There's even a place I can saddle up, mount and ride the hump on this fella's neck.

I know what you're thinking—why am I thinking this? Why haven't I dropped into a fetal lump, locked my hands behind my neck? Why aren't I on my knees, hands clasped in front, bleating out prayers, *Now, at the hour of our death*? Or madly digging to wedge myself, pig-tailed mole, into the earth? Why aren't I making an escape plan? Maybe I'm just too tired. Maybe I'm done. It's like the time my seventy-two-year-old mother, in the grip of dementia, went missing from her Medicine Hat apartment—I almost passed out, stumbled against her old, ugly, Hershey-brown fridge, though I had felt okay at the time.

With the bear, I don't stumble or faint. Not afraid at all. That's the problem. That's what holds me in place, this feeling of *not* feeling, this weird, I don't know, resignation (that's what Daphne always says at work, *I'm resigned to working here*, and I tell her *No, you can't resign, we work under the table*, and she laughs and says *No, we work across the table*, and we both laugh). As if a wave of true terror is a debt I need to pay to stop a bear attack. As if cold sweat or heart palpitations, or the feeling you get when you're drowning, ears and nose and mouth sewn shut, will be my payment for survival. That whatever strange force feeds this wilderness will know my fear and shake me free from the bear. And this big, shaggy-footed, goitre-eyed bear-god will vanish, poof! and let me go on my way.

Here's the thing—the fact that I feel no fear, but rather mild surprise, tells me the bear, in the natural course of things, will attack me, lop off my windy wonky head. Or, dissect me, if only to find out what might be buried inside such a foolish fearless creature.

The bear hasn't moved from his place. He keeps throwing his head from side to side, like a dashboard toy animal. But he ain't no toy. I know about bear attacks, have read grizzly accounts. I've never sought out such gruesome tales, but when you live on the fringe of Calgary, you can't help but hear lots of "human-meets-bear" stories, either in the local rags or from the other girls when we're lounging around, or hosing the place down, waiting for another guy to massage the buzzer.

Heard about a man who, riding his bike on a highway near Edmonton, training for the Tour de France, was dragged into the woods by a black bear, and buried, half-eaten, half-alive.

Story of a grizzly on the Alaska highway that, struck by a pickup, attacked the truck, limping off with the whole front bumper clamped twisted in his jaws.

And there's that poor bastard in northern BC, coming back to his hotel room after dinner, mauled right in the hall by a ghost bear—one of those white-phase black bears—that got in through a utility door that'd been propped open by some ditzy chambermaid.

Few summers ago, I read the bio of a woman who was mauled by a grizzly in Glacier National Park, her years of recurring nightmares, facial surgeries, painful infections. The writer, I found out later, killed herself in a Kelowna hotel room. I thought, hearing this, the poor girl should have died in the original bear attack, but slipped through the bear claws of fate, only to live a sort of half-life, bear mask fastened to her face. If it's your time, it's your time—no point trying to dodge the inevitable.

But even these stories don't stir me up, as if, rather than standing dirty face to face with a bear, I'm hearing about it second-hand.

Got to focus, start a bear inventory, study his claws. He has his big paws set gently in front of him, like he's waiting for a pedicure. Each nail is long, curved, elegant, not white as I expected, but the same rusty-car brown as his fur. Trouble is,

I don't picture what those bad boys could do. I try harder to be grim, grimace and squint, squeeze him with my eyes, find a family memory. Once, at Christmas, as Mom lifted the crackling turkey from the oven, the hot metal rack seared her arms. Bad part wasn't so much her burns, but how she howled at Dad that it was *his* fault, spitting, hissing at him as he fumbled a slab of butter from the fridge—*Bastard, how come you never do anything to help me*? Dad, butter-fingered, froze, like me beside the bear. Eventually he *did* move, got the hell out of there. I'm not thanking him for it. Left me and my brother behind.

I know pain might be coming my way—pain that would be like that, but worse, much worse: no butter, cold tap water, or soothing words can fix a half-eaten shoulder or a severed head. What if the bear opens me, yanks out my guts like wet laundry, spreads them on the trail? What might a magic, soothsaying bear divine there? A life of dullness and routine? A shitty life? *My* life? And if I can't sew myself closed, have to live with my insides blossoming out, like a new fall outfit, my slashed appearance at odds with the dreamy look on my face? Even these considerations don't do the trick.

Should I flirt with the bear? Maybe, posing in some goofy romantic way will help. Isn't there a book written about bear love? I once read a story about a native woman who, near a river by her village, surprised a grizzly. Guess what she did? Dropped her pants, spread her legs, turned out her best pink jewels. Said something like "Come, my husband, it is me," shaming the bear. Wouldn't shame your average man, though. Maybe I'll try. Or at least peel off my sweaty top, unhook my sports bra, drop it oh so slowly, flash the pressure lines in my shoulders. Purse my lips, bat my lashes, let my red hair down, wilderness Rapunzel. The thought of it might stop the beast, might also fire up something in my own heart. Or maybe the guy, if it *is* a guy, needs some solid R&R, just needs a bear hug, and big bearish rub and tug, whattaya think?

Another memory—I work at this place called Blue Therapeutic Massage. Guess you could say it *is* therapeutic, least for the guys. It beats waitressing up and down, that's for sure. I can make more in two days than in a week running off my feet, butting heads with rude customers and crude short-armed short-order cooks. And Rick, though he's a cock most of the time, is pretty good with letting us switch hours if we get sick onto death of servicing guys, and ... well, to the point. Month ago a customer asked me out. We don't date customers, but he'd been sweet and shy and the whole time he looked sad. I liked that. He was big, not bad looking, a bit Seth Rogenish, though a bit too hairy for my taste, furry-eared. Later, ran into him at the grocery store, averted my eyes like I do, but he introduced himself, asked if I'd like to have a coffee sometime, wanted to hear my story. They *always* want to hear your story. I said *No no, can't fella* and waved him away. He said he'd buy me some anyway, plopped this strapping feed bag of *Kicking Horse Dark Roast* in my little basket with a twenty dollar bill. Pissed me off. But the coffee was oh so good. Next week I saw him again, week after too, he just nodded at me, polite as all get out. But never saw him at the parlour again. Next time I saw him, leaning over the ground beef, I told him he could give me his number, maybe I'd call. I did call, left a message, invited him to lunch, wondered if I'd have to explain myself, how the job is just to pay the bills, that I want to paint, art school on my mind, though you don't need school to get good. I have my books, I got YouTube, I'm getting damn good anyways. Wouldn't ask him why he came to Blue Therapeutic Massage, not a mystery the way men are. Wasn't a mystery when he didn't call back. None of this matters, is the real story.

Real story is how I didn't care, one way or the other. Real story is how I wasn't hurt, and the thought of him calling didn't fire me up, either. And that's what's got me worried, that's why the bear not pulling any emotion from me seems part of a pattern, something I need to fix.

I start off again—think about my little brother Michael. He's the scruffy angel to unfurl his wings, to get me to *feel.* He'll be murdered by my loss. He'll be a wreck at the news I've been wrecked by a wild creature, in these mountains he hates (*Who needs mountains,* he says. *What purpose do they serve?*) All the times I defended him to Dad will come back to haunt him, all my arguing for his hand-to-mouth, hand-fluttering-to-cropped-head bohemian lifestyle, yelled at Dad while Michael grinned, whispered that he didn't need to *Justify anything.* Why can't I work up anger now? Anyways, Michael has long thin hands, all bone, skin translucent blue, like sleeping newborns, like preemies. When I look at them without looking at his face, while we sit in the coffee shop near his apartment, I pretend they're the hands of a very old man. Idea makes me happy in a sad way. Not the conversations or coffee, just his hands. Concentrate on his hands. But the emotions won't come. Even the idea of my baby brother's sadness, memory of his hands, doesn't awaken in me any horror at the dream of my own death.

The bear turns. Lifts his snout into the air, takes a step towards me. I hoist my sketchbook, the pages outfacing the bear, as if the bear might leave claw marks on it, a signature and bloody rendering. Drawing of a bear attack made by a bear.

Stops. Again, swings his head. Again, I see how *fine* he is—face wide and shy; ears pricked up; shoulders and hump gathered behind him, politely, like children waiting for permission to move. But I know he's a fur-coated bomb. I want, need, to draw him. But since I haven't done a sketch for weeks, I'm stopped by the deep layers, his depth, foreshortening effect like a Caravaggio. I focus on his musculature—I always begin with a subject's core, anatomy, have to capture his spine, his through-line. His *bearness.* For the first time I take my eyes off him, and sliding the pencil from my sketchbook, turn the open pages towards me.

I decide then, faced with the blank paper, and beyond that, the bear, his fur combed by a breeze, that nothing I can sketch can compare to what's standing before me. Time is the enemy. Time is a bear, big dumb lummox of a grandfather clock with bear ears, bear grin, tick-tocking, fur pendulum swinging. I'll never get the animal right in the time I have. Need to get away and remember. To wrestle with him, away from him, in peace. You know, *tranquility*. And, lo and behold, hallelujah! I begin to feel something, though it ain't fear—anger, mostly, for I need the bear to leave so I can paint him. The bear is similar to the job I have to make ends meet, what I do to survive. The bear is stopping me from getting on with things, from creating something that, later, might throw some light on my dead emotions. So, *ART*—all in capitals, underlined and italicized too, word bigger and stronger and furrier than the bear—is what finally moves me.

Is this bear creative? His talent might be shown in the way he kills his prey, in his attention to detail in maiming his victims. In colouring the high monochrome earth with stunned pieces of me, lending a new meaning to *fingerpainting*, to *brushstroke*. Maybe the bear's getting ready to turn me into a work of art, a masterpiece of killing, just as I need to escape the bear to give him life on canvas, to give *myself* life. Artist against artist, maybe, a standoff, better than that of Van Gogh and Gauguin. I know what I need to do. I have no other choice.

I'll give up my Art for the bear. I won't draw him, or even plan on drawing him, and he won't kill me. I love wonky things, but there's balance in this I like. I lift my sketchbook over my head, show it to the bear. He seems upset at the blank page, grumbles, rears up on hind legs. (Maybe it's an animal memory, the bear reminded, groggy hallucination, of a field of snow. Or maybe he's seeing Nothing.) I have the weird sense that he hasn't seen me at all. Perhaps I feel no fear because, hey, I don't really exist.

The bear drops, scruffs up dirt with his front paws. Coughs out a thin cloud of dust. Rakes the ground. Growls. Charges me. I do a little jump, try to pull my legs up inside me, press the open sketchbook against my face, blindfold for my execution. And the bear, at the last second, guard hairs tickling, kissing, dry-brushing me, veers off into the woods. Gone.

Later, I do paint the bear. After all, he really didn't keep his part of the bargain. He didn't attack me, yes, but he did maul my heart. In the weeks afterward, I still feel no fear, and there's no post-traumatic stuff, because I paint the hell out of that bear. I paint him up and down, forwards and back, tree-stump neck to stubby tail, attacking my canvas with oils. My baby brother Michael loves it when I show it to him; he eats it up, especially the bear story behind it. Says it's a great self-portrait—the mask-like face of his sister, the new artist, on the painted body of a charging bear. I name it: "Attacking the Bear."

I won't quit my job at Blue Therapeutic Massage, money's good and I've got art school in my head again, maybe next fall. Though when I try to hang my painting there, Rick says no, it'll freak out the customers. *They'll think they're here for a mauling not a massage.* Daphne agrees, though I argue, *Aren't they kinda the same?* I tell them I'll *resign myself* to their decision. Give the painting to Michael. Later, I call Seth Rogen again (his name's Don, but Seth would be better; he tells me he's thinking of changing his name anyway), ask him why he never returned my call. Tells me sorry, he sort of froze thinking about it, got scared thinking about how *emotional* I was. *You're shittin' me,* I say, then apologize and laugh and ask him if he'd like to go hiking in the Kootenays: *Just friends, no pressure, I'm going there to paint, maybe I'll paint you, no matter what your name is.* He agrees.

RUDY

WAS RELIEVED NO SMARMY BUSBOY HELPED HIM WITH HIS luggage. This was a more rough-and-tumble establishment, genuinely rustic: no busboys, no elevators, and the lodge itself like a small mountain, his room at the summit. As he carried his bags up the three flights of stairs, he was inspired by the stuffed heads he met along the way, pausing to consider each as he rested, nostrils pinching and flaring, on the sturdy, hewed-from-oak banisters: a snarling black bear that looked like an angry Tom Cruise; a placid bighorn sheep whose horns reminded him of the waterslides at an amusement park he'd visited the previous summer; and, above the third floor landing, an enormous bull moose, its antlers like ascending wings, creased and fissured and twelve-pointed. The moose's silent authority, magisterial look, was a reward for Rudy's conquering the stairs. And he expected, looking at its lifelike, shining eyes, that he might be awoken in the night by its gruff, disconsolate mating call.

He hefted his suitcases up the final rise of stairs, then down the hall. Whipcrack of wooden floors. His room number was fashioned from twigs, it looked vaguely deranged, vaguely *Blair Witch*, and the key he retrieved from the pocket of his khaki pants was a large antique one, the likeness of an antlered deer forged into the metal. Everything here was antlered. He was suddenly aware of his own head, how closely cropped his hair was. He wished he'd let it grow, connect to the shaggy net of hair on his back. He could have pledged his allegiance to Sasquatch, left all remnants of city behind. Hair and fur meant freedom.

Terrific room, appropriately appointed. Small but with the cozy sense of a cabin, features all torn, peeled and split, from the natural world: river-rock fireplace, wood-framed queen-sized bed, pine side-tables, a lamp whose spokes inside the walnut-coloured shade resembled whittled sticks. Even the mattress made a wilderness sound. When he tested it, there was an antique squeaking noise that he liked. It was a prodigal song about how he'd come to accept his own burliness, in a body that was wide, stumpy, though recently trimmed. His face, too, had a flatness, like a shorn tree. His eyebrows resembled curls of wood, shavings planed from a two-by-four. His face was Irish fair, and always got flushed in the heat, especially in Toronto's humidity. But here, or so he'd been told, there was no humidity.

He'd blend in with the forest. Something profound had stirred in him when, back home, he'd gone online to see the coloured photos of the Canadian Rockies. Something imprudent and energizing had moved through his torso. Something like desire, a peculiar longing like love, or whatever, for he wasn't sure what that felt like. But this felt good. He was forty-five, and no female since high school had tried to caress or kiss his pale face, or linked hands together behind his back. And yes, he was big enough to admit, it would be difficult to do that now.

Still in his airplane clothes, Rudy went down to the main desk to ask about trails. He'd start right away with something moderate, might even purchase a picnic box lunch for his adventure. But there were people checking in, two couples encircled by luggage: the couple at the desk elderly, in matching tan shorts and shirts; him with white hair poking from beneath his Tilley hat, and her with longish black hair, with twists of white. A younger couple waited behind them, him with muscular arms and crossbeam shoulders testing his purple T-shirt, her with burnished legs, though, in profile, she was silvery and sharp-featured, like a fully extended Swiss Army knife. She was stabbing his neck with her face. He curled one of his tanned arms around her shoulders, and she strained higher in her flip-flops. Rudy strained higher, too. He studied the splay of her fingers on the small of his back, thought how nice that would feel, a woman's hand on the small of your back. But Rudy's back wasn't small, and it didn't taper before it met, or rather collided with, his buttocks.

He snorted to dismiss this, then, ignoring the line, sidled up to the desk beside the elderly woman. As he turned to look at the young couple, his attention was seized by the old woman, whose gravelly but booming voice made him think, at first, she was talking to someone across the room: "You might consider going to the back of the line. Been here ten minutes. We're not *savages*, you know."

Rudy blushed, his face patchwork red. He snorted again, but this time it was a sympathetic, deferring snort, a half-snort, but it segued into a jokey tone that seemed to rub the woman the wrong way: "Oh, no, not butting in, just looking for a map. Guess I don't know where I am."

She didn't smile. The severity of her expression was emphasized by the shape of her eyebrows, the close ends of which thickened above her nose. She was a tad Sasquatchy herself. As he heeded her advice and retreated, the young woman unwrapped herself from her boyfriend and went over to examine, as he had earlier, the bison above the fieldstone fireplace. Rudy believed her contemplation of the animal was contrived, duplicitous, a concession to the immediate environment that was for the benefit of her companion, as if she were there to serve him, and as if he were an extension of the landscape, his arms and shoulders carved by the same glaciers that had done their work on the surrounding mountains. At once, Rudy loved and hated them.

HE FELL IN AMONG THE TOURISTS AT THE LAKE. EXAMINED THE ten peaks that marched across the sky. Wandered the beaten path on the lake's edge, passing groups of Japanese sightseers, most of whom hardly bothered to step aside when they encountered him. He took no offense, tucked his forearms behind him and continued, smiling in recognition of his own diffidence.

He arrived at a fork, one of the trails continuing along the lake, the other into trees. It was a trailhead with a bulletin board and a tiled wooden overhang. On the board was a map of the surrounding terrain, obscured where the plastic covering had fogged over, and this was obscured again by a big yellow laminated sign fastened there with industrial staples: *Bear Activity in Immediate Area. Hikers must proceed in minimum groups of four. Fines up to $10,000 for non-compliance.*

Way too dangerous to hike. *So be it.* Rudy was suffused with happy pragmatism, concluding that, really, he was in no shape to challenge the mountain. He was, like most the people around him, a "drive-through" tourist, was glad to think of himself this way. And he was content with his weight, had been inspired by an article he'd read in *O*, the Oprah Winfrey magazine, titled, "Welcoming Your Wonderful Outerness."

In fact, he was playing with the fat at his midriff, taking that bacon in his hands, jiggling it joyfully, repeating the phrase, "Hey, ladies, what's your issue, there's tons of me to love."

Earlier, he'd played the joyful jiggling game, then got sad—profound, big-man sad—and sat on the edge of the bed. Then, recalling the article's photograph of two large women high-fiving each other, and its advice about adopting a positive attitude, *Act enthusiastic and you'll be enthusiastic*, he'd laughed out loud, exaggerating the *huff, huff*, got up and stepped into his army-surplus shorts. He'd also wrestled on the mustard-coloured short-sleeved shirt that Liam, dear Liam, had bought him as a going-away gift, the shapes of two little black bears sewn into the shoulders. Now, back from his walk by the lake he decided, though he was tired, to have brunch in the lodge dining room.

Saw that he didn't need to hike. The designers of the lodge had brought the wilderness inside. There was, at the end of the dining room, a fieldstone fireplace similar to the one in the lobby. Beside it was a cast-iron screen corralling enormous fireplace utensils. Rudy was reminded of the westerns of John Ford. He'd read in one of his old movie magazines (he could never convince himself to get rid of them, they were stacked in neat piles twelve deep under his bed) that Ford always filled his movies with oversized props: huge frying skillets and spoons, big ladles and bowls for campfire or pantry scenes, outsized holsters, bullet-straps and pistols for the inevitable shootouts, and stagecoach wheels that stood the size of the leading man (often John Wayne), in the hope that all of these could match the Monument Valley landscapes, and encourage his actors to bring more passion to their performances.

Above the fireplace another bull moose presided, its antlers larger and darker than the one on the top-floor landing.

Running the length of the dark-panelled room were the stuffed heads of mountain goats, five on each side, white devils with sharp horns and spikey beards. On the fourth wall was a Native headdress, rainbow feathers on a train that was pinned out, the whole feathery expanse like an imperious but sleepy bird. It, too, seemed oversized, exaggerated for effect, a prize for some mythic Sioux Chief. Rudy felt a swell of pride that his own substantiality, his girth, was also a tribute to the landscape, like a prop in a John Ford western.

"Eggs Benedict," Rudy said.

The waitress brought a large square plate—another John Ford prop—the tower of food smothered in Hollandaise, with home fries that were charred black at the edges. The young waitress had chapped elbows and an odd, concave skull, forehead and chin prominent but her other features pushed in, all under a mop of brown hair that was too full for her retreating face.

She wasn't pretty. But Rudy was nothing if not forgiving, and he concluded that she'd had, up until now, a lonely existence. She poured him more coffee. He coughed and smiled and complained about his home fries, making it clear that he didn't blame her, that they were just symbolic of *the vagaries of life*. She didn't flinch, just lifted the silver coffee canister above his head—he flinched—while deftly removing his plate, eggs and everything. Her expression didn't change; her eyes didn't roll; she wasn't bothered or affected one way or the other. But he was offended, wondered why she didn't acknowledge his deferring tone; after all, his home fries *were* burnt, and he suddenly felt as though they were on a first date and her demeanour was telling him that, "You know, this is okay, but not worth pursuing. You're nice, and I've nothing against big, bear-like men, but there's just no spark, big boy."

He stared at his hands. Pulled them into his lap when he saw they completely obscured the placemat. He stared at the silverware. The handles of the fork and knife and spoon were little trees. He wondered if he could purchase the same in the hotel shop, they'd make a nice souvenir for Liam. Soon the waitress returned, and with one hand slid his plate back in front of him, curled the other behind her, in a sort of fencing stance. The potatoes were fine. But the top layer of egg and English muffin had slid off the stack, and the Hollandaise sauce looked angry, popping and bubbling. He could hardly complain that his food, while properly cooked, was aesthetically unpleasant.

He said, "Thank you so very much," letting sarcasm scorch his tone, his words charred at the edges, and smiled at the waitress, expecting one in return. Her face stayed neutral, and she held her strange fencing posture for too long, a theatrical pose that hinted at an irony that didn't jive with her expression. He began to re-assemble the collapsed tower of egg and muffin, aware that the waitress was watching him, convinced that she was standing in a defensive position to comment on how he'd complained about his food. When he began to shovel the corrected potatoes into his mouth, she disappeared.

He finished, left a too-generous tip, arranged the fragments of his home fries into a smiley face. He felt sorry for the poor, grim girl. Outside, he took the measure of the day: the rippling sky, the still lake, and the precision and ease of a family of ducks in a V-formation gliding over its surface, soft as a yawn. *They* knew the importance of aesthetics.

Already rent and spent, tuckered out, Rudy thought about napping, but wanted to save it for the mountain night. Decided he'd wait to savour the Hudson's Bay-blanketed bed; feel of the gnarly bars of the headboard; glacial breeze from the window.

Wait to be serenaded by the call of the wild, coyotes and wolves disappearing into their own ever-fading howls, like in the wilderness CD he'd downloaded in Toronto. Those animal songs had become the lullabies, soundtrack of his dreams, dreams that of late saw him stepping free of his bulk and floating in some small cloudlike mass that retained his substantial heart and—even casual acquaintances confirmed this—his wicked sense of humour.

On a bench by the lake, he fell asleep.

An hour later, he decided to turn in, though he knew sleep would come slowly. He'd prop his head close by the window so he could listen for his wilderness soundtrack. When he arrived at his door, breathing through his mouth, he heard laughter and turned to see, emerging from the landing, the young couple from the lobby. The man appeared even more robust from the front, and the woman was hanging from him like a torn muscle shirt.

Rudy saw, finally, the man's face, was surprised by it. His features were closely packed, like an owl's, and his chin was weak, sloping till it joined his protruding Adam's apple. Contributing to this owlish impression, he wore round, thin-framed glasses, and had a small, abrupt mouth. It looked as though his head had been placed on his body as a prank. The couple, passing by in the hall, had to push up against the far wall to avoid him. They apologized, *God, sorry, 'scuse us.* Embarrassed, Rudy looked down, saw the man's bulky hiking boots, dried mud in the treads, and the woman's red painted toenails in sandals. Her tiny feet resembled his own.

In his room, Rudy got momentarily stuck between the walls in the little alcove, nearly knocked down the picture there, a reproduction of a painting of a grizzly bear composed of tiny dots, like a pointillist painting.

Decided he'd sleep in his boxers. Got undressed, placed his belly's ridge of flesh on the edge of the pedestal sink in the bathroom. Studied the circles under his eyes. It had been, from his early arrival in Calgary, his drive into the mountains, and his hike, a full day, and he was feeling the jet lag. He decided to floss his teeth, retrieved the little plastic square from his toiletry case.

He unravelled the spool and wrapped the silky string around his thick fingers. Pulled the string right up above each tooth, massaging the root, even when this produced a trickle of blood. His dentist had shown him the correct method. But when he pushed his fingers in and began on the back upper half, the floss snapped, a piece caught there. Went to unwind more to dislodge the fragment, had retrieved only a small bit when the spool spun empty.

He tried to free it with his fingernail, but his nails were too short. He had a habit of biting them till they bled. Ran his tongue over the frayed string. Lifted his belly off the sink, let it return to its natural resting place.

Pulled back the blanket from the bed. Opened the window, stuck his head out and examined the terminus of the mountain. The air tasted like mineral water and smelled like a Christmas tree. Fell back. The clock radio read 9 p.m. Closed his eyes. Perhaps too early to sleep, but this sleep would be privileged.

Kept tonguing the shred of floss. Thought again of the *O* article, how one had to turn negatives into positives. The shred was the thin filament of a mountain flower, a piece of the wild, nestled inside him.

He began to hear things. Mostly silence, but silence with a particular quality: cold, strained, as if it might crack under its own weight. He'd never considered that silence might have personality. The wind picked up, like a train in a mountain pass, a plaintive sound. Then, a falsetto squeak, like an animal, maybe a coyote or wolf. He'd heard a wolf make such a sound in a documentary once, a momma calling her young to the den. The yips, yelps and squeaks grew louder and more frequent; they were animal-like, feral, but not exactly vulpine, and—Rudy was slow to realize—weren't coming from outside. A voice very clear, as if of someone next to him on the bed, said: "God, Ethan, rub it up, rub it up, rub it up, I'm coming."

Rudy opened his eyes, rolled onto his side, propped his head on his hand. Listened harder.

"Yes, my tits, my tits, take them hard, *hardest*, oh shit."

Rudy leaned over, stared at the floor.

"Ethan-oh, yes, *spend it, spend it all*."

There, what he hadn't noticed before: a wrought-iron heating grate, with little metal swirls, underneath a kind of plastic collar. He leaned farther, a cantilevered body. The bed screeched. Extended his hand and spread his fingers over the grate, trying to clutch the sounds. Pulled his fist back, smelled his own flesh, a sweaty, soapy mixture, with a pinch of burnt potato.

The voice kept going, from elsewhere, but *right* there, "Ethan-oh, push it in, *all the fucking way, in, in*."

These were not the wilderness sounds Rudy had anticipated.

He listened more, listened carefully, as if he was a participant. Felt a pounding in his head, as if his heart had ascended, planted itself behind his eyes. Threw off his sheet and blanket, hefted his legs over the opposite side of the bed, leaned forward before his belly stopped him. Waited for some cue, though he wasn't sure what his role was.

He went to the door. His bulk shifted, gathered hotly around the doorknob. Opened it and looked down the hall, concluded that the sounds were from the young couple he'd seen earlier, the thick-torsoed, owl-faced male, and the sharp, long-limbed female. Imagined her toes, like pieces of hard candy. He waited for a few moments, head outside, the bed sheet wrapped around him, expecting that other guests might emerge, confused, distraught, excited, brought up short from sleep, as if the hotel fire alarm had sounded.

Went back and stood in front of the window. But kept looking at the heating grate. Gathered the Hudson's Bay blanket from his bed, spread it on the hardwood floor next to the vent, placed one of his pillows there. Stretched out. Lost his balance, banged his forearm hard on the floor. Heard, for the first time, a man's voice.

"Was that you?"

The female voice answered, "Just, no. I don't know. Could we concentrate please?"

Rudy almost said, "I *am* concentrating."

Then she said, softly, but still loud enough that he could hear her breathing between the words, "Rub it up, rub it up. Oh, fucking right, rub it, Ethan-oh, oh."

After another twenty minutes of the sounds, "Oh, Ethan-oh, rub it up, pinch again, rub it up, take it," etc. Rudy got up. He was surprised how long they were at it. The woman kept promising but *wouldn't* come; perhaps these hardy mountain types did everything in extremity, the hiking and the humping. He was amused but bothered too, this was something else he'd never considered, like the quality of silence, but in this case he didn't care. He gathered the pillow and blanket and lay crossways on his bed so his head was near the windowsill. Slammed his eyes shut and tried to pick out mountain sounds, to separate them from the moaned urgent words. But Rudy didn't hear coyotes or wolves or even the wind in the trees.

Eventually he descended into sleep that was anxious, afflicted, kicking the tangled sheets, punching the feather pillows, thrusting his tongue between his teeth, against the piece of stuck floss. Swam arduously into sleep, struggling upstream. Felt his body was working harder than it had when he'd walked along the lake earlier that day, or when he'd dragged his wine-coloured suitcases up the three flights of stairs.

JUMP-STARTED AWAKE AT 6 A.M. DOSED. ROLLED OUT AFTER 10:00. As he dressed, holding the waist of his pants open before him like a hoop, he felt unbalanced, as if his top half had emptied of something.

In the dining room he ordered a BLT. The same waitress served him, but she was different. She moved slowly and smiled broadly, and her eyes brightened when she brought him his sandwich and home fries. *She's prettier today,* Rudy thought, unhappily. He joked that his home fries looked *Perfecto* this time, and she continued smiling but didn't respond. She didn't seem to remember him.

Revitalized by his lunch, he decided he'd try once again to get a map of the local trails, sure the hotel staff could recommend ones that didn't require a minimum of four hikers. But the front desk clerk was occupied, this time with two dames dressed to the nines in Goth, all corseted, black skirted and lipsticked, their heads almost resting on one another's shoulders in whispery conference. Rudy was tempted to ask them if *they* knew any good trails, but assumed they weren't local, were part of some film shoot or modelling assignment, so just nodded. The Goth girls didn't notice.

Rudy decided he'd try to get information from the hotel gift shop and, anyway, he needed to buy some floss so he could dislodge the piece still wedged between his molars. The gift shop was closed. A small, handwritten sign said, *Back in five minutes*. Rudy waited ten and nobody came. He went out onto the dirt trail, but didn't care to retrace his path from the day before. He walked towards the road that corkscrewed into the valley. Came upon huge slabs of rock, limestone and shale, a stone dam at the terminus of the lake. Scrambled onto its lower shelves, found a good place and decided to sunbathe, though he didn't like the sun. Wedged himself between rocks, a fragment of human floss in the teeth of stone.

Remembered that the vista before him used to be featured on the Canadian twenty-dollar bill. Wished he had one, wanted to compare it to the real scene. The image had been slightly Victorian and had the feel of a woodblock print, so unlike the images on contemporary bills, and so unlike the images he worked on at the design firm. He couldn't quite conjure it and kept seeing the bright, colourful lines of the new Canadian currency. He felt this acrid nostalgia, imagined himself on the back of the old twenty, wearing a fringed buckskin jacket and paddling a canoe, like Pierre Elliott Trudeau in a famous photograph, drifting into some clean, symmetrical version of yesterday. He unglued himself from the stone slab, picked his way down, avoiding the shouting children who were using the pile of rock as a jungle gym.

He went back to the gift shop but forgot to buy the dental floss and the map of local trails. Instead, he purchased a Moraine Lake snow globe, a set of placemats depicting the valley, and a reproduction of a vintage postcard of the scene he'd been contemplating, a black-and-white image that had been colourized. It reminded him of the old twenty.

Spent the rest of the day examining these artifacts. Set up a little shrine on the dresser. Kept shaking the snow globe, hoping, somehow, the stingy wash of flakes would increase and coat the tiny landscape. The day passed. He found himself in a fighting mood as the light began to fail. When he'd entered his room, he thought he smelled the woman in the next room, an aroma like hot chocolate. "I'd have plenty of whipped cream on that little number," he laughed to himself.

DARKNESS CAME, AND SO DID THE SOUNDS. THE SAME moaning, the same phrases that Rudy had repeated in his head that morning as the waitress was taking his order, "Rub it up, rub it up, push harder, harder, fucking right, Ethan-oh." This time, Rudy responded in the opposite way he had the night before. He propped a pillow on the window ledge and lay down, his head in the open air. He didn't want to miss any *real* wilderness sounds, his overdue welcome. Just as quickly, he abandoned this hope. He arranged his blanket and pillows on the strip of floor beside his bed, his head by the grate. He extended his ear like a hand.

He was nothing if not a discerning listener. In fact, he noted a difference in the timbre of the sounds. Though the woman used the same phrases, there was less urgency, a world-weariness, or an over-rehearsed quality, that suggested that something had come between the couple, that there was a rift in their relationship. Specifically, the woman's deep, throaty exhalations had moved up to the front of her mouth, had taken on a commanding curtness. Perhaps the young couple sensed their privacy had been compromised.

There was disappointment in how the woman said the words, "Oh, Ethan-oh, rub it up, rub it up." Rudy felt bad now, angry at how things had changed. He wondered why the man didn't address the issue, challenge the woman. His annoyance allowed him to relax. Their lovemaking was imperfect, incomplete. For the first time on his holiday, he felt contented. Bad and glad. He drifted off to sleep, curled like a newborn around the heating grate.

Morning, and Rudy thumped down the hotel stairs in his new hiking boots, blew by the black bear, the bighorn sheep, the moose. He'd slept well, had woken up in bed, couldn't remember the point in the night when he'd moved. He felt renewed. Perhaps sleeping part of the night on the hardwood had cricked something back into place that had long been out of alignment.

On the last staircase step, he misjudged the height. His buoyant mood didn't prevent him from stumbling. He caught the last section of the banister, righted himself. Looked up, deft in his clumsiness, saw the couple from the next room lacing up their hiking boots, on a kind of Shaker bench to one side of the buffalo head. The man's forearm muscles bulged. The woman mirrored him.

Neither of them had noticed Rudy's stumble, as if they couldn't deviate from a military routine: the tightening of boots, hoisting of backpacks, and how they both ran their hands down their bodies, smoothing out lumps. They were streamlined and ready to go. But Rudy knew different. Nevertheless, as he strolled by them, he felt, in contrast to their lithe precision, overstuffed and awkward. Paused near the entrance to the dining room. Heard the woman say, "Let's push ourselves, the Pass is supposed to be spectacular." It was *the* voice, for sure. Her partner said, "Anything that wakes me up. Then we'll need to check out now."

Rudy wouldn't have to listen to their lovemaking again. Felt a stab of regret, and concluded that their leave-taking was indeed evidence something had come between them. Perhaps he could help them. Perhaps he could lock onto a new mission. Perhaps his presence here was fated, but had nothing to do with the landscape. Maybe the call of the wild was entirely personal, and involved some intra-species bonding and repair. But he *was* in these mountains, and decided he could touch both the human and animal, the human and the environment, the mountains that loomed and invited him on all sides.

HE LINGERED NEAR THE TRAILHEAD, SETTLED HIMSELF ON A log that straddled two stumps. Found himself truly occupied, concerned with his feet that were pushing up against the inside toes of his boots. At the store, they'd felt great. His feet had swollen. He yanked the boots off, felt his socks. Removed them and smoothed them flat, parallel to one another on the log. Placed his puckered feet on his boots. They resembled two bullfrogs.

A fivesome of hikers blew past. He pulled his feet back, watched the parade of rope-like calves. These were serious hikers. If he followed them on the trail, he would learn a new way of looking at himself, bolstered by their rigour, their energy. He could float in their footsteps, like a baby wolf. He let his feet emerge from under the log.

The man and woman finally appeared. They strode up silently, the woman in front, the man hard behind. Just beyond Rudy, the man halted, rocked back on his heels, lifted an arm towards the yellow sign. The woman stopped, swung around in a tight, impatient way and said, "What's wrong?" Rudy hid his feet again.

Ethan-oh dropped his hand, lifted it. "This," he said. "*This* is wrong. There's a bear. Have to hike in groups of four."

The woman grunted, bear-like, laughed and said, "Yes, well, great, fuck that. Are we gonna get arrested? Let's go, we'll be done before mid-afternoon."

"$10,000 fine. These park wardens, this is how they make money. I don't want to be the one...."

The woman turned away, faced the ascending trail, said, having interrupted him with her movement, "Yeah, Ethan, I get it, but I still don't think. Shit, I drove all this way, paid for the room…."

"Plenty of other hikes. What about the Plain of Six Glaciers?"

"Chickenshit. I say we take our chances. We'll say we didn't see the sign. Better to ask for forgiveness than permission."

"Won't enjoy myself if I'm worried."

"Bears aren't a problem. How many bears have we seen in all our trips?"

"No, worried we'll get caught. Remember what I said about being discreet?"

"Yes, I get that, but this? Million to one."

Rudy kept his eyes down. When he looked up, the couple were staring at him, having noticed him for the first time. But Rudy was used to people's double reactions, though they usually occurred in reverse: first they'd recoil at his largeness, as if his weight represented a personal inconvenience, then act as if he didn't even exist.

The woman approached. Rudy dropped his eyes again, watched her boots, her ankles, her knees, her waist, her hands on her hips, and where her flesh-coloured T-shirt bulged. Didn't look at her face. Too late, he realized she might think him rude, a typical male sizing her up before making eye contact.

"Excuse me, sir," she said, "are you planning on hiking this trail, Sentinel Pass? Are you finished, or waiting for someone, or looking to join a group?"

Rudy was confused by the multi-pronged question. He looked up, and for the first time saw, full on, the woman's face. It was cartoon-like, every feature outlined and stylized. He became aware of his own exposed parts: the veins in his wrists, wisps of hair in his ears. All were tingling. The woman was attractive, but in a stony, inflexible way.

"Yes, but the sign," Rudy said. "I was deciding what to, ahh, one person would be too conspicuous, I was trying…"

He stopped. He wasn't saying what he wanted to say. He didn't know what he wanted to say. He hadn't thought this through, realized his vague plan was … vague. He wanted to help this couple, but how? Or did he? Maybe things, maybe things would work themselves out. *Arrange* themselves. He was thankful the woman cut him off.

"Sure, we could hike together." Then she turned a bit, looked at Ethan-oh, got a look of qualification.

Ethan-oh said, "Still only three of us. The sign says …"

"For God's sakes, Ethan. I'm sure we'll run into other hikers."

Rudy said, "Yes, some hikers went by, not ten minutes ago."

"No worries then," the woman said, looking at Ethan-oh. Rudy noted that Ethan-oh's face hadn't relaxed. There was something else, some problem, though if the woman was willing to ignore it, so was he.

Rudy worked his socks and boots back on. Ethan-oh came forward and, as if confirming their agreement, offered him a hand. Rudy blushed at the look of surprise on Ethan-oh's face at the effort it took to pull him upright. Ethan-oh suppressed this, turned around in time to see his lover disappearing on the trail's first rise.

Before they'd gone fifty yards, Rudy had fallen behind. Ethan-oh kept slowing, trying to appear as if he, too, preferred an easy pace. Each time he paused, he stepped to the trail side and crouched, as if examining some flower or rare insect. The fourth time, he stood and turned his back to the forest and introduced himself formally, wiping his palm on his T-shirt before extending it.

"I'm Ethan. That's my wife Connie that's abandoned us."

"Rudy. You guys from around here?"

"Kamloops. Come here couple times a year. Where you from?"

"Toronto. I can see why, it's beautiful."

"No arguin' that."

Conversation was hard. It might be better, Rudy thought, if folks never spoke, could just overhear one another.

Ethan-oh was nodding but looking at the ground. Rudy understood why. Sweat was bubbling on Rudy's forehead, streaming into his eyes, stinging them, making him blink. Ethan-oh waited before continuing, wiped his own brow in sympathy with his new sweating friend. "You're staying at the lodge? Think I saw you there. If your room is only half as nice as ours, must be nice."

Ethan-oh was pushing the toe of his boot against a tree.

Rudy said, "You don't need to wait for me."

"No problem. Seen mountains before. But I *should* keep up with Connie. Don't want to end up one of those animal heads in the lodge."

"Go ahead. I need to tighten my boots."

Ethan-oh raised his hand in a partial salute, as Rudy decided that his lie about his boots was true. He sat, untangled the thick diamondback laces. Yanked his foot free. Aroma hit him that reminded him of pasta on the boil. Peeled the sock back. It was fastened to his big toe, glued there by blood. The nail of his big toe had folded inside itself, scissored his flesh. Instead of listening to Connie and Ethan-oh the night before, he should have been trimming his toenails. But he'd trimmed them back in Toronto, couple days before his flight. How'd they grown so quickly? His feet were the least of his problems. Wondered if his lungs were also bleeding, riddled with rents, unable to contain his violent breaths. His internal organs were tumbling together, like clothes in a dryer. He'd rest for five minutes. Things would get better once he'd acclimatized.

He was determined to keep his part of the bargain. He was one of a threesome, had agreed to it. He was *connecting* with these people. He would, through his presence, help them deepen their own connection. His slowness, they had to understand, was a choice. This wilderness was new to him. Needed to contemplate it at his leisure. He eased his sock back on, his boot, pulled the laces tight so he couldn't pretend they'd loosened.

Their tightness would change his life. He was pulling everything tight, no more excuses. He got up, led with his waist, wouldn't think about anything except what propelled him forward, and details of the environment: a broken tree, zippered with insects; a tree stump as flat and wide as an altar; and a beam of sunlight as bright as an apotheosis. When he turned to catch his breath, it was truant. He blinked rapidly, caught glimpses of the ten peaks, snow packed in their ramparts, their majesty diminishing as he ascended. But he *was* ascending.

His goal was, rather than to finish this hike, to keep pace with the couple. It was obvious that Connie had only included Rudy in their threesome to pacify her husband, Ethan-oh, concerned with the law. Perhaps he was also the sort of person who needed to play the Good Samaritan, a contrite and ashamed penitent. Ethan-oh was the one, after all, lagging behind to accompany him. Perhaps Rudy was fulfilling, in his lumbering personhood, some need of Ethan-oh's. Connie would appreciate this. And, later, if he managed to keep up, he could claim a sort of reward, meet Ethan-oh and Connie for a drink in the lodge dining room.

They'd share stories of their adventure. They'd laugh and lift their beer glasses and luxuriate in their familiarity, glad at the knowledge of who they were, surrounded by the heads of all the animals. The waitress would see that Rudy wasn't alone, and her concave face would rise, come out to meet him. They'd go upstairs together. His night wouldn't end in solitude.

His resolutions slipped with every step. Mountains didn't care about resolutions. His legs were monolithic. He envied the mountains their stasis, their indifference. Began to pretend he was on the treadmill in his condo's fitness room. He'd tried it once, and had gone just below the ten-minute mark before he'd been forced to program a slower speed. The landscape was moving past, trees and more trees, all the forest gradations: fir and spruce, pine and birch; the many pretty flowers that Rudy wished he could identify; and the creeping vines and lichens that chained things together. The trail was a tunnel pointing upwards. He was climbing, yes, he was climbing, *Rub it up, rub it up*. He'd be rewarded for this, one way or another; he was emailing Ethan-oh and Connie from Toronto, complaining about life in the city; he was planning another wilderness trip, could he stay with them in Kamloops? Connie would, over dinner, look at him with affection, this portly but attractive man who'd challenged himself, despite his weight, his disadvantages. Trees and more trees. It was fortuitous they'd stayed in the same lodge. They'd have no secrets between them. Connie would help him get his weight down to 200. Ethan-oh would gain weight as he aged. His wife would admire Rudy all the more and he'd begin to date again. And Connie would hint, Ethan-oh smiling, going along with it, that she was jealous, that it would mean Rudy would be spending less time with them, that their lives would thin out, turn insubstantial.

He couldn't see the trail. He was gasping. He said to himself, *I'm gasping*. It sounded like an Olympic sport. He could join the gasping team, no problem. He stumbled off the trail, straddled a tree, fell into the crux of two branches. After some time, his breathing slowed. Eyes cleared. He didn't know if it had been a few minutes or an hour. The trees were shorter here. Light poured onto the scene and his degradation.

Caught a glimpse of colour ahead. Inspired, he launched himself. Then fell backwards onto his pack. Could hear voices, but the words weren't clear, just a random and anxious nattering, like Canada geese. Felt a new weight, realized it was a hand on his shoulder. Ethan-oh was saying, "Sorry, man, you don't look good. I'm sorry, we shouldn't have continued. This isn't a life or death thing."

Connie's face came close, distorted. She lifted his arm like a deadfall, worked his numb fingers around a bottle, said, "Drink. Rest. Be better if you went back. One of us will go with you. Be the best thing."

Rudy closed his eyes, slurped from the bottle. A sound filled his head like a tractor breaking ground. Still felt Ethan-oh's hand. Could feel Connie kneeling in front of him. Then, a feeling of well-being. It was their concern, their love. He loved them, too. He really did. He wanted to tell them, wanted to tell them that they loved each other. That they should *always* love each other. He wouldn't let them down. He'd pushed himself and been rewarded, said, "Is this the end? How much longer?" He opened his eyes to find Connie standing, her kneecaps level with his eyes.

"Well, no, partner," Ethan-oh said as he joined Connie. "We're about a quarter ways, if that. Haven't broken the tree line."

The thinness of the forest had been temporary, a bald spot on the mountain. Or perhaps Rudy's exhaustion had razed trees, as if he'd inhaled them. Still, his serenity remained. Perhaps, this was the signal he was acclimatizing. He didn't know. He was in uncharted physical territory. He'd never pushed himself before. It was strange, terrible, exhilarating. He wondered if sex were like this.

He said, "Let's go. No worries." Aware of himself again, he kept his eyes on Connie. He knew that she knew he was watching them. She wouldn't look at Ethan-oh. She said quickly, "Don't think that's a good idea. Nothing personal, but. You probably need to try something easier."

She stood there with a look of cold practicality, like a mother being calm and reasonable with a dim, unreasonable child.

Thoughts were pounding in Rudy's head—*Something easier*. Why? Easy is overrated. *Nothing personal*—this was something a woman said once she'd disembowelled you, and you stood with your steaming intestines in your hands.

"I'll go down with you," Ethan-oh said. "I mean, you'll be okay. But we feel bad."

Ethan-oh saw something in Rudy's face, stopped talking. Rudy was, at that instant, picturing Connie's painted toenails.

He said, "Thanks, 'preciate it. I'm fine now."

Connie turned away, straightened her backpack, unclicked the plastic waist belt, clicked it back into place, looked at Ethan-oh and said, "Nothing personal, but I, *we*, don't want to be responsible if you, you know, have a coronary."

The dream was dying. Was writhing like a beast in the dirt. Rudy looked at Ethan-oh, grinned, laughed, grinned too much, looked at Connie, looked at Ethan-oh. Ethan-oh shrugged and said, giving the beast a final kick, "Sorry man. Maybe we'll see you back at the lodge. Good luck, then."

Connie continued. Ethan-oh tried not to hurry, to make it clear he felt no guilt, that he didn't need to distance himself from Rudy too quickly. He swung his backpack off, let it hang from his arm, adjusted one of the straps, lifted it again, nodded at Rudy and said, "Sure you don't want me to walk you down?"

Rudy's face tightened. "No need," he said. "Not quitting. I'll be right behind, all over you like a cheap suit."

"*Suit* yourself," Ethan-oh punned, then made the sounds of a snare shot and cymbal crash. Rudy didn't laugh—pun or no, it was a phrase Rudy disliked, no good ever came from it. Ethan-oh continued, then, his backpack bouncing. In a moment, he'd disappeared.

Ten minutes later, Rudy collapsed onto the tortured trunk of a limber pine whose blunt branches jutted over a precipice. His limbs had fused together. Couldn't balance himself. He was a tree whose roots didn't penetrate the earth, but remained near the surface; given a little breeze or radical notion, he'd fall. He imagined that Ethan-oh and Connie had detoured into the woods and were fucking there, excited by their encounter with such a sad creature, that their own strength and desire had increased in proportion to his fecklessness. They were propped against a tree, Ethan-oh penetrating Connie from behind, shorts around his ankles, and the pattern on her dropped panties blending with the forest floor, skinny pole legs white against the greenness. Rudy had read somewhere that human beings are the only species that makes love face to face, so Ethan-oh and Connie were contradicting this, obviously of some lesser species, bereft of dignity.

SUDDENLY, OR PERHAPS MUCH LATER, RUDY WAS LOOKING AT Ethan-oh and Connie. They'd returned. They stood before him on the trail. The sun was falling and they were backlit, features washed in shadow, their heads sporting wild halos. He was glad he couldn't see their faces. He thought, for a moment, they'd returned to give him a chance to regroup, but the pounding in his throat, his homicidal pulse, told him otherwise.

"Look, we want to help you. We'd feel better if you let us walk you down."

Connie looked at Ethan-oh and continued, "We'll see you down. We don't mind. We can hike again tomorrow."

Rudy recognized Connie's tone of voice. It was a tone he knew well. It always went with words of charity, forgiveness. He was being forgiven. But he didn't know what sin he'd committed. And she was lying. They *wouldn't* be hiking tomorrow. They'd checked out. Why was she lying? He didn't need their pity.

He let his backpack slide to the bottom of the tree he was swooning against. His shirt was plastered to his skin. His head throbbed, and he began to shiver so severely that he spoke in retaliation, as if the words might settle him: "Oh, Ethan-oh, rub it up, rub it up, rub it up. My *tits, take them hard, harder, rub them up, oh, Ethan-oh*."

Ethan-oh and Connie didn't speak or move. Rudy decided his tone wasn't desperate or angry, but playful, familiar. He stood up and, plugging his hands into the pockets of his khaki pants, spoke again. This time he looked right at Connie.

"Rub it up, rub it up, oh, Ethan-oh. Spend it, *spend it*, push it *all*, the way *in*."

"What?" Connie said. "What are you saying?"

"You know, you know," Rudy said. "Last night, *last night*, it was *so* good, rub it up, rub it up, push it in, all, all the way in."

Rudy had a thought, then, an idea that hadn't occurred to him before—maybe Ethan-oh and Connie *knew* he was listening. Maybe the distance he'd perceived in Connie's voice the night before, the rehearsed quality, was because they were performing for *him*, in some perverse ritual. Perhaps they enjoyed, as a kind of foreplay, tormenting the fat boy in the next room. And maybe their asking him to join them on this hike was an extension of this, the climax of a planned humiliation. His aloneness was offensive to them, so they'd conspired to assault it, to assault his privacy, in a kind of cruel prank that reminded him of school days, although this prank was of an entirely new order.

Rudy said, then, almost spitting, and pulling fists from his pockets, "Rub it, rub it, rub it, rub it up, *fucking Ethan-oh, goddamn fucking good fucking great fucking all all the fucking way.*"

Rudy could see their faces now, as if some light had turned on inside them, or the sunlight was penetrating their heads. He let himself continue in the tumult of something he didn't understand. Perhaps, this was what lovemaking felt like, this rush, this abandon, the words flowing freely, this sense of going too far. The contempt in Connie's eyes didn't deter him. In fact, Rudy imagined this was part of a negotiation. After all, sex was about anger, too.

Ethan-oh looked at Connie. Connie looked at Rudy, back at Ethan-oh. Ethan-oh let his backpack drop. Connie whipped her hand forward, grasped Ethan-oh's wrist. The rope of their arms tightened, snapped. Ethan-oh was striding purposefully towards him, all his facial features spread apart, the owlness of his face set free.

Connie shouted, tried to stop her husband. Rudy took a step back, half-turned, tripped on the pack he'd let drop by the tree. He let himself fall, all his exhaustion on this day gathered in that moment, all the sleep of which he'd been deprived, all the times he'd merely watched, listened to, the lives of others. He fell heavy and hard, a tree uprooted, flesh avalanche. His shoulders cleared the twisted trunk of the pine, but his face met it with full force, jolted his head back until his body yanked it under the tree, onto the precipice. He lay there, stunned, emptied, satisfied.

Ethan was beside him now, grasping his arm. He said, "Watch your head," helped Rudy into a sitting position. Connie was there, too, and had his other arm, was stroking it. She jumped up and said, "I've got some gauze in my pack." The throb from earlier had become more specific, was pulsing in the side of his face. He leaned forward and spit. Blood and saliva splattered onto his pants.

"Whoa there," Ethan said. "Let Connie get some gauze."

Rudy saw, floating on the stain of darkness on his crotch, a tooth. He reached out, lifted it by a little cord, the floss that had been wedged between his teeth. The sight of it and of Connie kneeling before him, and the heat from Ethan's hand, made Rudy mad. He lurched forward, startling them, spitting blood into the dirt. Swung his head from side to side, like a bear trying to identify a scent. And he knew what he was trying to identify—Ethan's intent, what Ethan would have done to him if he hadn't stumbled. The unknown of this hurt Rudy more than the pain in his face. Or, rather, it was the tremor of a notion: the idea that Ethan had come at him, *not* with violent purpose, but to hug him a big, manly, bear-like way—the same way Liam sometimes hugged him, that lately made him suspect that Liam's affection for him was more than platonic—and to lend him some comfort in his humiliation.

He spit out more blood. It came out in strings, in cords. He clambered to his feet and mumbled, his mouth not quite working, "Jus leave me lone, fuck off. Need to be lone."

"You're hurt," Ethan said. "You need help."

"Don't," Rudy said. "Leave me lone. Fine. Go, leave me lone."

He drew out the O of alone, in a long, soft howl.

Rudy grabbed his pack, started down the trail, tilted,

steadied himself. Connie strode after him. She offered up the ball of gauze. It was a softer, bigger version of his tooth, a white tail dangling from it. She said, "Take this, it'll stop the bleeding."

Rudy was angered by her reasonableness, her kindness, her presumption. Nothing would stop the bleeding. He snatched the ball of gauze, thrust the whole thing into his mouth. He'd done enough talking anyway.

ALONE IN HIS DESCENT, RUDY THOUGHT OF THE BEAR IN THE vicinity. Wondered what he could do to attract it. He wished he'd splashed on more cologne that morning, that he'd been aggressive with deodorant. Or that he'd purchased a box lunch from the dining room. He could stop and languish. Could lie down and balance a meatloaf sandwich on his chest, let the aroma waft into the woods to bring back the grizzly on its leash. It'd lop off his fat head. His head could be stuffed and mounted, set on the wall in the lodge, among other animals. He'd listen in on conversations. Strangers' eyes would flit over him without judgment. He could be inside and intimate forever.

His face shuddered. He felt as though he carried his own palpitating skull, tucked under his arm. His other hand gripped his tooth. He was relieved he'd not lost it. He'd already left too much of himself on this mountain.

Just as he began to think about the hotel waitress—fuck her, he'd dine somewhere else that night—a woman stepped out from the trees. She appeared at the side dulled by his injury so it seemed she'd just materialized. He almost dropped the tooth. He turned his good side towards her, and she took hold of his arm. He recognized her—she was the old woman, the Sasquatch woman, half of the couple he'd seen at the checkout desk two days before, the cranky one who'd scolded him.

His shoulders bunched up. He didn't want her help. Then she said, with some urgency, "Look at this." She guided him off the trail, into the trees.

He followed the trajectory of her arm. It took him a moment to discern, in the spackled forest, what he was seeing—between trees, illuminated there, the tall white tail and speckled hind-quarters of a deer. Its snout bobbed up and down, tongue flicked in and out. Grooming a tiny fawn. The smaller animal was turning its head, closing its eyes, occasionally stepping forward, back, on tiny, uncertain legs. Rudy had never seen a deer close its eyes. He didn't know that he didn't know if a deer *could* close its eyes. Did deer sleep? He hadn't thought about it. How could they, in their extreme vulnerability? And did they dream? What kind of rich, soft, floating landscape might constitute the world of a deer dream? Did other deer bound through, antlered, golden, never touching down? Or had he inherited this image from Disney? What did he know about nature? His mother had once described *Bambi* to him, it was one of the tragedies of her childhood. Perhaps a deer dream was more a nightmare. The world was a cruel cruel place.

He tried to focus on the scene again, just as the fawn stumbled and the mother propped it up. He wanted to shout, *Enjoy it while it lasts*, knowing a bear was nearby, would make short work of the fawn if the mother got distracted.

The woman, who hadn't released his arm, squeezed it again and said, "Beautiful eh? Doesn't get any better than this." She whispered the words close to his good ear, his good side. Her hand touched the small of his back.

She guided Rudy onto the trail. She shifted, stood in front of him. "Oh *my*, you all right? What happened? Got an awful bruise on your face."

He thought of asking where her husband was, or at least the man she'd been with. Why was she hiking alone? Hadn't she seen the warning? But she'd turned again towards the trees, towards the doe and fawn, reluctant to break away, as if she'd located a necessity in this vision, a key to something, as if something in her life depended on it. Rudy could feel her longing, or loneliness, or happiness, or fear, he wasn't sure which. Then she said, Rudy detecting some sadness in her tone, and as if she was relieving him of the burden of speech, of explanations, "Take *care* of yourself. Better have that attended to. You're not far from the trailhead. Thank you for sharing this." And she was gone.

Rudy considered dropping the tooth, sowing it in the wilderness, from which might grow, what? Another *him*? Maybe a smaller version. Or maybe, mixed with this soil, something new, a sort of listening tree, whole world onto itself but a common feature of the mountain. He decided to keep it, tuck it under his pillow. Couldn't remember ever doing that as a child. And yes, he'd have his face attended to, among other things, many other things. Squeezed his tooth so tightly that, when he arrived back at his room, it'd made an impression, a small, irregular imprint on the map of his palm.

THREE PLACES

I AM HERE TO BURY HANNAH. HERE TO BURY MY WIFE. She wanted to be buried where the river meets the shore. I'm here to scatter her ashes. This is one of the places we visited some twenty years ago, on our honeymoon. Even up until the moment of her death, she would say, "Don't forget, Jack. Don't ever forget—take me to that river." Bow River. Here I am.

In her last weeks, she hardly spoke. So her last request has heft to it, more than a last wish. We didn't talk much, over the years. Just lived together. Together, yet apart. It's the *apart* part, I know, that interests you. Contentment is not interesting. Desirable, but not interesting. We had some measure of contentment. Mostly, not talking. Getting used to not saying anything was a form of contentment. I learned to be content. I learned to not say anything.

She was set in her ways. She was always singular in what she wanted: routine. She built a life from it. Our life. Even our vacations would alternate in predictable ways. One summer, we'd drive to Lake Huron. Spend days on the stony beach near Bayfield. Drive from one bed and breakfast to another in Goderich, or Kincardine, or Exeter. It was always Southwestern Ontario. Alice Munro country. And every other summer, we'd indulge in some extravagance. Fly out to Calgary. Rent a car. Drive into the mountains. Stay in Canmore at the same little boutique hotel with the yin-yang design in the carpets and the crescent-moon-shaped windows. We'd do the same hike every trip. Hannah would pack a couple of ham and Swiss cheese sandwiches, two Oreos, and two orange juice cartons with the little, bendable straws. When we'd get tired, usually halfway, we'd turn back. Stretch out on the hotel balcony. Read. She liked mysteries. She'd read Agatha Christie or P.D. James—mostly the same two authors, alternating between them.

This went on for years. Two places on the agenda. Two places to visit and come back to. But when Simon, her silent yet brash brother, got ill, Hannah wanted to be close to home. Before Simon died, we spent a summer in the city. That was fine. That was that. Unfortunately, he died badly. He wasn't very good at it. Hannah wasn't good at accepting his death. At least, his burial. Then routine set in again. Two places. Here and there, back and forth. One time, when I suggested Europe, she looked at me as if I'd slapped her across the face.

Even in our domestic life, she didn't like change. A place for everything and everything in its place. For instance, she couldn't stand dishes in the sink. But she didn't like dishwashers. No matter how taxing the preparation or meal, while I loosened my belt and reclined in my chair, she'd be up doing the dishes. That image of her, vivid: the back of her neck, white as chipped porcelain, her short, brown hair curled inward, her shoulders working. The dish rack filling up in precise order, row after row. She liked to get right to it. She liked to get things right. It wasn't because, sitting across from each other at the kitchen table, we didn't talk, though we didn't. We were okay with that. It was because the sink should always be clear. That's what she'd say. Little aphorisms or statements that sounded larger than the words. "Sinks must be clear." Or, "Never go to sleep in an unmade bed." And I'd nod. Or go into the living room and put on my slippers. She bought me slippers for my birthday, two pairs—red plaid and brown plaid, one pair for upstairs, one for down, in case I was in either place and had forgotten to put them on. Each floor taken care of, no worries, and no cold feet, up or down.

When she cooked, the meals often alternated between pot roast and pasta. Both dishes could be reheated as leftovers and served on a system of staggered days. I'd make the occasional pot of chili, or stew. Or we ate out. In restaurants, we always sat side by side. When I was younger, I never understood those couples that would sit shoulder to shoulder, rather than across from each other. I always thought it was because, being old, they had nothing left to talk about. Or they didn't need to look up and see that same pair of eyes, that same shrinking mouth. Now, I understand. It's not out of boredom. It's fear. Fear of death. Neither of you wants your back to the room. It's strategic. You need to see what's coming through the door. Facing the room, returning to Bayfield, or to Canmore, to the same mountain view, like a comfortable pair of slippers. Avoiding Europe. You know where you're going next year, and you know you'll be alive, as if death might feel presumptuous about interrupting so ordinary a pattern—two places, here and there.

"Bad things happen in threes." This was another phrase she'd utter, when hearing the news of some tragic event. Even when we began to date, things were predictable. Nicely so. Lock step. Two operating as one. When she pushed for this or that restaurant, this or that movie, this or that concert, this or that position in bed, I always deferred. She was strong and knew what she wanted. I was happy to slip into that mode. Happy to yield. "Two to tango," she'd say. I'd blink twice in agreement.

Before I met Hannah, I'd been vanishing. When I fell in beside her, I felt bolstered up, significant. I reappeared. She always knew where she was going and was always prepared. She even carried toothpicks in a Ziploc bag in her purse. Would wield a toothpick and put it to work after dinner, even in a restaurant. I never complained, though sometimes I'd excuse myself and hide in the restroom until she'd done. Her teeth were big. People saw her teeth before they saw anything else. At first, I was embarrassed by her teeth, her horsey smile, those two, big front teeth coming right at you. But, in bed, I liked watching them. Her mouth looked like it belonged to someone else. After she died, it occurred to me that we should have had a separate funeral for her teeth. I thought of the folklore or vampiric legend of burying teeth to watch what would spring from them in the burial ground. I never shared this idea with anyone. It was a funny thought, and also not funny. I never joked about her teeth when she was alive.

There were some strange things about her. Some unusual things. One time, on a dusty Sunday, she wanted to go to the CN Tower. Out of the blue. She'd never mentioned the CN Tower before. I thought we both shared a silent contempt for it. When I asked her what was up, she said, "Never mind."

Another time, while shopping on the Danforth, she stopped on the street to talk to a homeless man. Gave him a twenty dollar bill. Asked him what kind of day he was having. How old he was and did he need a warm sweater? She'd never talked to a homeless person. I can still see her crouched, sitting on her heels. After, when I asked her why she'd chosen to talk to this *particular* homeless man, she misunderstood and said, "How could you ask that? How can you be so unfeeling?" I didn't try to explain. And it never came up again, seeing as, whenever we'd encounter other homeless people, she'd just stride by them, arms pumping, looking straight ahead, as if all the other homeless people existed in another mysterious category of homelessness.

Hannah carried a handkerchief, a large one she'd launder every couple of days. It was her father's handkerchief, had his monogrammed initials, XK. I don't remember ever seeing her father use it. He was a man who never got sick. He was a big man, six foot five in his stocking feet. I got a crick in my neck when he came by. Always wore a suit when he visited us. Made our furniture look cheap. After he was gone—that is, gone for good: high cholesterol, high blood pressure, the burden of grief—she began to use his handkerchief to wipe down the chairs we'd be sitting in whenever we went to either of our favourite restaurants. Wiping down the chairs, her furious circular motion, was an occurrence as routine as the mechanism of sitting, or how we'd sit side by side.

"Take me to that river," she'd say. "Crack that bugger open on the bank," she said, towards the end, "and scatter my ashes where the bank meets the water." It sounded poetic. I liked the way it sounded: *where the bank meets the water*. Two worlds coming together. Sometimes, I thought she wanted to go to the Rockies just to look at the rivers. The mountains hulking overhead, their solidity, made the rivers seem wilder. "Where the bank meets the water," she'd say. There was no argument.

I had to quit my job to come here. I had the week off for the funeral, but Bob Parkin was already on holiday. He'd gone to visit his daughter in Oxford. She was there on a scholarship. And Peg Stackhouse was taking time off because her young son had Crohn's disease, had to have surgery. So we were short-staffed. They didn't want to give me the time to go out west, to scatter her ashes. Wanted me to go to a book conference in Prague. Asked if I could wait. Suppose I could have.

But I was fed up, anyway. All these stories, the mountains of manila envelopes, the writers' efforts to get right inside characters' heads, the effort to dramatize various lives, the details, the descriptions, the dénouements. Why? It all seemed so tiresome, so invasive. Sometimes, the chicken scratch or scrawl on the face of the envelopes contained more pathos, more sense of the author's personality, than the writing inside. Maybe, I should have been an agent for poetry instead of fiction. But there's no money in poetry. Precious little in fiction, anymore. Hannah's paycheque was always double mine, though she never complained.

We had practised safe sex on our honeymoon, with the promise of wilder things later on. It was a promise never kept. I don't remember the Bow River. Remember walking and holding hands under the grand smirk of mountains. My mind was always racing ahead to what we'd do that night. I felt as though I was pulling her along. I had to get somewhere, somewhere physical. We never had children. Never discussed why. I thought that something might happen on its own. I thought she might surprise me. But she never stopped using birth control. I remember examining the strange plastic case on the bedside table, each pill in its tiny compartment. We got older. The guest room stayed the guest room, that gun-metal colour. Nothing changed. No children.

We did things, of course. Though she didn't like to talk about movies after we'd seen one. We never went to plays, or operas, or museums, or art galleries. "Too immediate," she said. "Too right there," she said. We liked to have lunch in restaurants. In Lady Marmalade, or at Okay Okay. And she always wanted to sit near the windows, in the light. "I want to see my food," she said. Whenever we'd eat out in summer, it was always on Okay Okay's patio in bright, scouring sun.

She'd chew with her face up. Top lip peeled back. I'd hunker down beside her, squint at my plate. I began to bring sunglasses whenever we'd eat out. I took to wearing a hat.

It had been a routine doctor's appointment. Some pain in her back. She thought she'd pulled something. They found fluid in her chest. Lung cancer. They told her that she had less than two years to live. We got a second opinion. It confirmed the first. She hadn't smoked a day in her life. After the diagnosis, we talked. But mostly, she talked to Edgar. She always went to see him when she was through with me. Edgar is gay. She'd known him for years, had met him at art school. He's a glass artist. And he looks like a stained-glass saint, sharp-cornered and thin. I imagine light can pass through him. And he has a high whinnying laugh that would always send shivers through me, as if I were the one about to splinter.

I don't think she was happy with me, at the end. Maybe she was happy, before that. I don't know. I was happy, anyway. Sort of happy. I had nothing to compare us to. Okay, I did have something to compare us to. I'd been married before. But that hardly rates. My first wife was bipolar. One day soft, and the next day hard. When she was soft, she got involved with another man. It was more my fault than hers. We were only together for three years. We were young. It seems like a dream, now. Or, a dream within a dream: two dreams trading places with one another. I really didn't understand her. One thing that stands out from that time; she told me that once, when she was a little girl, on a driving trip with her parents, she'd seen a pair of dead white horses on the highway. A semi had hit them. I'm not sure whether this was something that happened to her, or was just a dream she recounted on one of her hard days.

On the night of the diagnosis, Hannah cried. Never heard her cry again. Not even at the second opinion. I don't know why she didn't cry. Maybe, she'd spent all her tears on her dead father and brother. I wished I'd asked. But I wanted to respect her privacy. One time, as we approached the big cemetery where her father and brother were buried, she said that gravestones look like human fingernails. That all the graves are like fingers sticking up. I liked that image. She said, "I don't want to be buried. Scatter my ashes." Then she said, "The dead don't know anything." It sounded like an accusation. I said, "What could they know?" She looked at me as if she had an answer. But that was the end of the discussion.

I'm standing on the bank of the Bow River. I'm holding the urn with her ashes. I'm standing here holding her. I don't want to move. Don't want to unfasten the lid. Feel as if I'm comforting her. I feel as if I'm holding her hand. I crack off the lid. Scatter some of the ashes on the river, where the bank meets the shore. Where the water washes up and soaks the edges of the weeds. I stop. I stop, though I can hear her instructing me. Light washes the mountain. I look up. It's silent, but the mountain has a secret to share. I decide the Bow River isn't enough. I decide something else. *The dead don't know anything*. I'm agreeing with her.

I hike up the mountain. Follow a trail. It's hard going. My heart throbs in my head. Sweat gathers behind my knees. I'm not well equipped. My running shoes slip on the rock. I trip over stumps. I don't make it all the way to the top, not even close. Still, there are bits of snow in the shady parts. Gnarled trees that look like bone. I find a little clearing by the trail and dump some of her ashes there. A little pile. I descend again and return to the river. Look down to where the river meets the shore. Take off my sneakers and socks and roll up my pants and wade out. The water is cold. It burns. I scatter the rest of her there, in the middle of the river. Not where the river meets the shore. Straight into the water. Where the water is never the same. The ashes make a little web there, for a moment, where the pale water flows fast. Does she know that I've buried her in three places? One is the place she wanted. The other two are not. No more arguing with the dead. If she were alive, standing next to me, she'd be angry. I'd move towards her anger, ghosting her, mouthing, "The dead don't know anything." And she'd repeat it back to me, as if I hadn't spoken at all.

MARILYN IN THE MOUNTAINS: NINE POSES

In August of 1953, Marilyn Monroe travelled to Banff and Jasper in the Canadian Rockies to film River of No Return. *She was obligated to make the film, nearing the end of an exploitative seven year contract with 20th Century Fox, and was unenthusiastic about the project. The director was Otto Preminger and her co-star, who would receive top billing, was Robert Mitchum. The cast stayed at the luxurious Banff Springs Hotel, and Marilyn, during the shoot, was visited by her soon-to-be husband, retired baseball star Joe DiMaggio. John Vachon, a staff photographer for* Look Magazine, *was assigned to document Marilyn's stay in the Rockies and took a series of photographs, many of which did not appear until 2010. This piece is a response to the idea of Marilyn in the mountains, a response to some of Vachon's photos, and a re-imagining of others.*

1. MARILYN AND THE GRIZZLY

It's beauty and the beast, of course. But I can't help imagining, beyond the frame, the photographer and a room full of men, packed in amongst the taxidermied animals, antlers, stuffed flightless birds, beaver pelts tacked to the white plank walls in the Banff Indian Trading Post. I think of the men stuffed too, immobilized and anxious, fur on their tongues, not sure exactly what they want, but that they want to save her. But it's me wanting to free her from the nightmare of history, letting my words ride up against the dusty frozen mass, thawing mastodon, everyone around her.

I'm sure she saw the irony, the grizzly's elbows on her shoulders, her right arm curving to sooth the beast, her eyes on the raised grizzly paw—the bear a kind of heavy necklace or bullying fur she might wear to dinner that night. Yet the moment is routine, another photo shoot, another pose, another clot of men. *Another* is the word that rends her heart, that bites her from the inside, makes a raw meal of her expectations. She hoped to get some rest here. Both men and women go silent at her appearance, glum, dumbstruck, wanting to equal her fame with something said, to touch her, somehow, in order to touch themselves; their expectation like a grizzly in the river, scooping out its own reflection, or maybe the long turquoise claws of the northern lights.

The photographer would like to pull her out of the bear too, a wilderness magic trick in photographing her. He misses his chance—she steps free, moves beyond the bear, beyond the room, her shoulder raised against the camera, and against the men who, like clouds, drift and separate, dissolve against the antlered walls.

2. MARILYN AND THE WAITER

The head waiter swings in like one of the swallows outside the windows, on an arc of cool air. He balances so many things this day: Marilyn Monroe and Joe DiMaggio, Otto

Preminger and Robert Mitchum, and two lesser men ready to order, though Mitchum makes them all wait, his menu balanced like a butterfly on two calloused hands. The rest of the staff whisper and crane their necks in the kitchen in a Busby Berkeley line, though the waiter glides unaffected, hotly professional, trying to demonstrate exactly who he is, set against this celebrity.

He waits, breathless, for a telltale sign: the edge on a laugh, a cough, slice of humanness. Really, he's a voyeur seeking who he used to be, when young. Marilyn accommodates, drops her napkin and twists to retrieve it, bends and slides her injured ankle out from beneath the table's apron (one photograph of light and flesh to be preserved or set among less elaborate dishes; one shooting star ranging across the cold turret sky; a river erupting between Celtic standing stones; one memory rippling out across the restaurant like a holy pealing bell—but the photographer, at another table, can't nail the moment, forbidden to shoot during dinner). Marilyn plucks the cloth in a quick arc, shakes her head at something her director has said, pauses then steps back, cautious as a fawn, into the river of conversation. And the head waiter breathes again, over the velvet spread, row of red desserts.

3. EDGE OF THE WORLD

No lights in the valley. The hotel is set in the side of Sulphur Mountain, ramparts and walls overlooking trees and water. When night comes, the hotel blazes. Beyond, the darkness intensifies.

Marilyn feels it when she and Joltin' Joe DiMaggio retreat to her room. DiMaggio pries his long shoes off, flops onto the bed. He's decided he's no slugger, wants to escape from the memory of swing and crack, triple and home run. But he's on deck with how she looks.

Marilyn goes to the window, *I wanna see how we're situated.* She also wants to step free, from the flashbulb and scoop, and the deep flyball that won't come down. She makes a gesture towards this, drags back the curtain, gasps at the view—nothing. Nothing at all. *It's like we're at the edge of the world,* she says, facing the night. And, as if she must form solidarity with that void, plucks some tissue, starts to claw the makeup from her face.

DiMaggio, face down, doggy nose in the pillow, doesn't understand. She keeps her back to the bed and him, trying to adjust, testing the shutters of her eyes, as if some light might flare where no humans are, where the river is alive but invisible.

4. THE WRANGLER IN LOVE

There was something democratic about her.
—Carl Sandburg

Monroe's the river, Mitchum's the mountain. That's what the Russian wrangler thinks, holding himself and his horse down, his leather skin cracking with effort, badland flesh running with new fissures, ornery black lightning bolts. He's more right than he knows, but won't groom his metaphor any more than that, won't bring it to a gallop. He knows his job, though something flares inside him, watching them prepare for another take—Monroe with her fingers on the ledges of her hips, Mitchum blowing cave-sized smoke rings, Preminger burying head in hands—some twinge of injustice about geography, about the way the mountain looks down, coldly dominates. But he knows, too, that the river will crack into tumult not far from here. He puts his teeth to the saddle horn, bites and bears it, as if someone's prying a bullet from his thigh.

Later, he'll crush his horse between his legs, gallop hell-bent onto the mountain trail, the world throbbing below. He can control or at least understand this, the horse's head a compass point. Or the horse's neck like a tunnel, glistening throat of a diamond mine. He digs right in, shovelling sweat, snatches of blood, hair, whiskey, bone, riding far away from her, his dream of democracy, what he knows will drive him mad if he stays.

5. MARILYN AT POOLSIDE

She injures her ankle during the shoot. Nevertheless, the photographer, with his editor from *Look Magazine*, decide a bathing-suit session would be sweet, even more so now, Marilyn on a cast and crutches, yet determined (they're dreaming of copy) that she won't let this stop her from enjoying the pool, competing with and completing the water and sunlight with her hair and her skin. And once she settles into a chair by the edge, straps of pink plastic squeaking her bum, she obliges a line of young women with autographs. They wait and fidget along the deck, along the trajectory of her suspended leg, flashbulb waves below them.

But these slim, snake-haired stenographer girls aren't awe-struck or dumb, and they're a bold bunch, conferencing here at the *Banff Springs*. They know how any hard surface might swell and cover her whole body, like lava, hardening into darkness. How her calf-itching cast might creep up to suffocate her. They don't really think this. But the idea is contained in how each of them, after, with a mean wink, and reducing their eyes' apertures, tucks the famous name away.

6. MARILYN AND THE WHITE-TAILED DEER

A deer darts across the Banff-Jasper highway. But the Brewster bus hardly slows—the driver is a veteran of leaky edges. Marilyn slides tight to the window but doesn't speak. The driver believes she's charmed by what she sees, moved by that grace and fragility, the deer thin as river mist. The photographer, half dozing, looks up from his Leica.

They're all wrong in what they're thinking. Marilyn doesn't daydream or sigh, doesn't coo at the innocence. Instead, she's appalled at the blink of fur and flesh, how it vanishes without upstaging the light; without dragging a back leg like a dancer floating in ecstatic delay; without pausing to pose, to wink at the ton of bright metal bearing down. Marilyn wants to sympathize, but in a flash just as full, fleeting, and dangerously antlered, hates that deer right inside the trees.

7. ON THE SKI LIFT

He has to steady himself to get the shot, balanced on the beard of scree that keeps shifting below his feet: the loose rock, the mountain where it's fractured, tumbling towards the river. And, too quickly for his liking, Marilyn slides into view, riding a thin wedge of wood, suspended by a bar and singing cable that seems to link earth and sky. The ski lift in summer. Publicity stunt. But in his mind, he snaps a different photo, a sort of Man-Ray, surrealist image: the whole ski lift as infernal film projector, reels whirring and spinning, and carrying a terrified miniature Marilyn helplessly through its teeth and, finally, in front of the searing light. And, indeed, in the glare of mountain sun, Marilyn appears to shimmer and burn. But she materializes again when she clears the treeline. He flatters himself in believing that he's outside of it all, and he's not far wrong, slipping on the shattered earth, avalanche in which ragged clouds might gang up to pulverize him. But Marilyn has the upper hand, at least for a moment. As she passes, she smiles and throws an arm into the air, gives him his money shot, free in the knowledge that the mountain is more than any of them: more than the black thread trying to bind it; more than that gangly photographer straining to hold it steady; and more, even, than the light that, every day, leaves it to fend for itself.

8. RIVER REMAINS

She wears dark green to match the mountain. Strolls out from the wood-burning fireplace cabin, takes in the river. Takes it in—begins to float on this meditation, a carpet woven of care and sadness, a strong weave. But there are more bumps than on the water, more peril. Flinching, she smacks at her sleeve. Emerald dragonfly stutters off.

She snaps herself out of it, looks up. Thinks how she doesn't know the mountain's name. Keeps only one impression: that whoever names it will hold a mountain in his or her mouth, like a new tongue, like the one carving the south side of the sky, named for a heroic World War One nurse: Mount Edith Cavell.

Last, she settles her gaze on a glacier, white mortifying bed. Christens it *Norma Jean*. How many names will she need before she becomes a mountain? She flutters her hands, tries to brush it off. The Athabasca River remains.

9. LOOK

Why can't you look with equanimity at a woman who's not your own?
—Yelena, from *Uncle Vanya*

She'd like to try on the river, or perhaps the crystal sheen of trees—yank the skin of a birch up along her wrist, forearm and shoulder, then button the knotholes. Mostly, she'd like to unclothe herself, peel the flesh from her bones and do a complete reno, graft a mountain onto her milky neck, dam the flow, then take a circuitous and recalcitrant tree root and screw it into where her spine resides. She wants to disappear into this place, have it disappear into *her*, its reach and rule and steadfastness.

In Vachon's final photo, she rides in a water-smooth Crestline Convertible. She fords the stone bridge, smiling and waving to the riverside crowd. Her waves are little heartbeats or, more precisely, palpitations. Tourists jostle and shout. She steadies herself as the road splits and wishes she could look at the mountains in a new way. *How would I play a mountain? Or river? What does the wilderness want? How does it feel?* But the mountains seem like nothing more than white-haired southern gents, pushing up the continental divide, mailing out their invitations.

But she keeps one photo for herself, outside of the spread in *Look Magazine*—outside of the hotel, swimming pool, car, and cabin—a hidden photo, undeveloped, unknown, a selfie from 1953: Marilyn in the mountains, alone, when she broke free from the bear and crowd that day, waded in the river's shallows, glad at the cold clarity, the pins and needles, her puckering feet new-born things on the carpet of stone and light.

FROM CASTLE MOUNTAIN

1

Banff Internment Camp, Cave and Basin, Banff, Alberta, Canada, December, 1916

SENCHAK LIFTS THE HEAVY PICK, SWINGS IT ONTO FROZEN ground. Shivers scare through the surface ice, making an arrow in the direction of the wide part of the clearing where, for the first time in days, sunlight scratches through the overcast. He ignores it—thinks of hissing but the mist might freeze—and swings again. Catches rock. Blade screeches and bounces off. He feels a flame in his wrist, a fire in his right shoulder blade. Lays the pick alongside his leg and looks up, the rest of the men in a loose circle within the wider circle of trees.

At intervals, one of them lifts and drops a shovel, or hammers the ice in quick succession. *Full hopeless.* And anyways, too much time is spent, Senchak thinks, with the men tugging off gloves, one finger at a time, like society ladies, and blowing into their pain-scorched hands.

A man named Petriv slams his shovel into a sloping white crust then comes towards him, wedging his hands into his armpits. *Hands always in armpits.* Tucks his whippet head into his raised collar. *Makes house of coat, this man.* Senchak puts his gaze on the work crew and keeps it there, even when Petriv addresses him in their native Ukrainian.

"Can't see point," Petriv says, leaning in the direction of the guards. "Crazy to make us fight ice so."

Senchak doesn't answer. He removes a glove, sticks a thumb in his mouth, sucks then examines it. Blood frozen around the fingernails. Says, still not looking at his countryman, "Better than sleep all day in bunkhouse, no?"

Petriv follows Senchak's gaze to where it empties in the direction of a break in the trees, a swath in the relentless march of spruce and fur up the mountainside. Earlier, a cow moose blundered out from the opening, smelled their ragtag group and loped back into invisibility, followed by a lone thin wolf that also halted, lifted a bald snout, bit violently at its own starved, protruding ribs, corduroy road. Bolted before any of the guards could take aim. Senchak wonders what became of the moose. Flexes his hands—they're murdered too, whipped raw, stiffened in the shape of the pick's handle. Finally, Petriv answers, says, "Yes, better." His voice is too loud, as if he's using the words to vanquish some daydream.

One of the guards, Private Ramsay, whose broad face makes each of his features appear stranded, nears. Petriv props his head back, stretches his arms in mock ecstasy, or crucifixion. "Might want to get your back involved," Ramsay says. Petriv snaps up, blinks rapidly, says, trying to find the correct words, "Earth like iron. Listen to it, like bells fat on New Year." Senchak reaches for his pick. The guard flinches and steps back. Embarrassed, he steps forward again, circles back with forced ease towards the prisoners, approaches Private Kemper.

They talk, heads almost touching. Senchak listens, though some of the words are unfamiliar.

"Like pushing glacier," Ramsay says. "Prisoners right to complain. Why not wait till freeze breaks?"

"Petitioned for transfer," Kemper says, his high cheekbones so raw they look flayed, like carved meat. "Can't spend the war here. Can't piss without rootin' to the ground."

Kemper removes one of his gloves, blows into his fist. Ramsay aims his rifle butt at Petriv, who has wandered away from Senchak and back among the other men. "That one's peculiar. Malingerer. Like to ram my barrel up his ass, for *mo-ti-va-tion*."

As if bolstered by the sentiment—threats provide a kind of heat—one of the other guards, a large Irishman named Window, so nicknamed because he has a reputation for blocking the view, comes over and sits on his tree-stump haunches, greatcoat sweeping the hard snow, rifle balanced on his knees. Despite his crouch, his head is level with those of the two guards. Kemper ignores the giant and says to Ramsay, "Go easy. We'll head into town soon, imbibe prolifically. Maybe the whiskey'll thaw my toes."

"Aim to fall down drunk, stay that way," Ramsay says.

Window says, his coal miner's voice big and coarse and bison-dark, "You boys not current? Two privates court-martialled for that up Jasper way. Drunk on duty. I wouldn't if I was in your boots."

"My boots'd burst if you was," Ramsay says. He and Kemper laugh, their laughter turning into quick, shivery hiccups. Window doesn't react, so Ramsay adds, "Kiddin' Window. I don't drink, hardly. But a court-martial would be a ticket out of here."

Kemper says, "Best watch our tongues. Heard weird stories of cold so bad that words freeze, and whole conversations thaw out in the spring."

The three men lift their eyes from the group of half-frozen ethnic Ukrainians onto Mount Rundle. The tilted mountain resembles a howitzer. But the wind that has dressed all the trees in stiff white long-tailed shirts rises and sears their eyeballs, sure as hot coals. All the men, common in their misery, hide their faces. Not Senchak. He extends himself, raises his pick, drops it with a crack like a rifle shot, startles the others. His shoulders ache to go ahead, go ahead, and he pauses only to will, to will, that Petriv will follow his example.

2

Over Eastern Canada, May, 2008

I'M A WHITE-KNUCKLER, WHEN IT COMES TO FLYING. Never thought about what that phrase meant, *white-knuckled*, till the first time I flew, crabbed my fingers under the armrests, drilled my heels under my seat, as though I was outside the plane and hanging on. Especially on takeoffs and landings, or in turbulence. I imagine the cabin depressurizing, expanding like a small doomed universe, big mushy skull. Or we'll explode in a midair horror, a Cessna off course, drifting into our flight path. Anyways, don't like it. But Dad, sitting next to me, is gloomy but fearless, and I blame him for my fear, my continuous pre- and post-flight nightmare. He's perpetually bitching about the stupidity of his fellow man, and the cruelty of fate, and the galling unfairness of just about everything.

I read an article once that argued that the young are concerned with justice, the old with mercy. Not Dad. He doesn't correspond in any remote way with this, seems to have lived his life backwards, more bitter now than when he was younger. I can't picture him without the question mark of white hair sprouting from his widow's peak, or his scowl.

Hasn't hurt his appetite. On the plane, he eats everything. Before I've peeled my applesauce cup, he's polished off his whole tray: the weird salmon shepherd's pie, stale hockey puck roll, the mini apple cake (where do they *make* these things, there must be a miniature bakery somewhere, rows of tiny pans and measuring cups and raccoon-like hands furious and fastidious on a shrunken, flour-flecked assembly line). I tell him he looks crazy, fish flakes on his chin. He doesn't wipe them away, but catches them on his fingers, licks them up.

"Small food," he complains, so loudly that heads turn. "Not enough for a cat. Should have taken VIA. Too slow though. Once, goin' to Montreal, train stopped for two hours, wouldn't tell us what the delay was."

He opens the little wrapped oatmeal cookie I gave him earlier, takes a niggling bite, drops the crescent moon into his shirt pocket, not wanting to waste anything, and determined—and this is *it* with my dad, this is the crux of everything, the crux of him, if you like—to get everything that's coming to him.

"No good way to travel," I say, trying to calm things by agreeing, also nodding at the young woman across the aisle, who gives us an annoyed glance every time Dad speaks. She has cold blue eyes in a white, doll-like face, eyebrows thread-thin and black, but our eyes meet and she softens. She understands that I'm just as bothered by my father's complaining.

With irritation reddening his neck and hairs curling against the collar of his red plaid shirt (I've told him he needs to get his barber to shave him there, guy he's been seeing for some thirty years, probably stone blind) he says, as if responding to something I've said, "Wrote to Harper. Still haven't heard back. Sure it's in some slush pile. Nobody reads letters anymore. Japanese got compensation, why not us? Dad wouldn't stand up for himself in that regard."

I don't respond. I'd hoped to avoid the topic till we got into Calgary. Don't remind him again that Paul Martin, during the time he was Prime Minister, pledged a couple million dollars to fund memorials and educational exhibits commemorating the internment of Ukrainians during World War One, and that the pledge *has* been put into action. Of course, we won't see any money, but why should we? My grandfather's incarceration was almost a century ago. I try to re-frame the discussion—I know, not really a discussion, this blurting out, this perturbed and tiring exchange of words—thinking of the landscapes ahead of us.

"Dad, you'll like the mountains. Remember when I came here with the debating team? Wanted to come back ever since."

He lifts his food tray above his head, anxious for one of the flight attendants to take it. The empty containers threaten to spill off onto the person behind him. I put a hand on his arm, "Dad, they're busy, be *patient*."

I nod at the woman again, roll my eyes. She grins in support then doesn't. I'm losing her. Dad says, "No desire to see mountains. National Parks. Can go to the beach, look at the ocean for free."

"You'll like them," I try again. "Sure, even your dad thought they were beautiful."

"We're not after beauty," he says. Lifts his tray again, eyes straight ahead and arms raised. Looks as if he's being robbed.

3

Banff Internment Camp, Cave and Basin, 1916

THE SIX NEW GERMANS SIT TIGHT TO THE WOOD STOVE, hands out, opening, closing them near the flames. Their faces are both wistful and severe, all the men in the camp recognize the look, but there is something peculiar, too. *Spit of a look*, Petriv calls it, an arrogant pinch, though Senchak knows that Petriv is supplying this, further to his reaction from earlier that day, when the Germans first arrived. While most of the men fell back or drifted to the sides, Petriv stepped up, spat on the wooden floor, slapped his forehead in mock salute, clicked his heels together, made a reference to *Der Kaiser*. The Germans didn't speak, but Senchak noted how Ramsay ushered the newcomers towards the bunks at the end of the bunkhouse, though there was space near the Ukrainians. Still, the rumour had arrived before the Germans that they hadn't been required to work at their former internment in Vernon.

Private Ramsay reappears to announce that the road work has been delayed due to the "intolerable" temperatures. Shouts of relief, though not among the Germans. *Evidence*, Senchak thinks, *that they have not yet broken their hands*. When concern is raised over the dwindling wood supply, the small group of Romanians volunteer to slash and chop away up above the Cave and Basin, despite the murderous cold. Senchak, although recognizing the Romanians' play for advantage, doesn't volunteer. The bad blood between Petriv and the Germans compels him to stay behind. Just as he guessed, no sooner have the Romanians filed out of the bunkhouse, mummified in blanket coats and grease scarves, than one of the Germans, a man named Kessler, walks over from the circle around the east end wood stove and towards Petriv. Cross-legged on his bunk, Petriv examines a silver locket and doesn't notice the German approach. Petriv always takes the locket and chain, Senchak has seen, from an inside pocket of his threadbare vest whenever he settles into his bunk, unclasps the tiny door of its face and stares at whatever is inside. But Petriv won't reveal the contents, despite the fact that many of the men routinely contemplate pictures of loved ones and think nothing of sharing, of smiling or perhaps not smiling, of bragging or perhaps not bragging over these images, though they rarely speak at length of their lives that were put on hold. Senchak never asks what is concealed there, though he assumes it's the image of some woman, perhaps Petriv's wife. He amuses himself by imagining her to be a smaller but more robust version of Petriv, and her cradling him like a child. He believes that one day he will share the image.

Kessler, shuffling between bunks, pauses over Petriv, who is fully bent over the locket, its small silver chain coiling around his wrist and fingers, like a rosary. Upon hearing the German's voice, the guttural snap, "What's that, jewellery on you?" Petriv turns, swings his legs over the bunk, unravels the locket chain and deftly slides his treasure inside his vest. He places his hands, black under the fingernails—though his hands are not yet broken, *Not sufficiently broken*—on the edge of the bunk. His shirt tightens on his neck and shoulders.

Senchak listens, perched on the end of the next bunk. He has some sense that the German is only trying to make contact, *Breaking the ice*, as they say. He also knows that Kessler, apparently the leader of the Germans, is obliged to be provocative. He doesn't want to risk the scorn of his countrymen.

Petriv finds no softness in the German's tone and says, "Leave me lone. Guards vill bring you fancy German cake and silk glove to keep soft your hands."

The other Germans shift from their positions around the wood stove. Their shadows increase on the bunkhouse wall. Kessler doesn't take the bait, just nods and sits beside Petriv and answers what he thinks are the implications of his words.

"You believe in work? Work hard, fingers to bone, yah. We are criminals then, not prisoners. Maybe you criminal. You work hard maybe to forget. Why you working, I ask? Making road for country that imprisons you?"

"You reason vee here," Petriv says, with a motion of his arm.

"Did nothing," Kessler says. "Had land, new land. 20 cents acre. Good land, Bruderheim land. Making new home. Next, war is on. Next, RCMP taking me. Who started war, *not Kessler*."

"Vie you telling to me?"

"What jewellery for then? Trade for freedom? Picture of woman inside? Or Prime Minister Borden you love?"

"*Yah*, Prime Minister."

Senchak stands then, steps closer, waits at the foot of Petriv's bunk. Kessler finds himself between the two Ukrainians. Senchak keeps a neutral expression, says, softly, picking the words as best he can from the Queen's English, *This is all not-ting*. He knows the five other Germans have also moved closer, although they too stand easy, perhaps agree, *This is all not-ting*.

Kessler rises, brushes off his pants and wool jacket as if something has dirtied them, turns towards Senchak. He nods when Senchak steps aside to let him pass. Senchak sees that the man's face is discoloured, a flame-like cloud staining a portion of his jaw and neck. Once he's gone, and the Germans have gathered again around the wood stove, Petriv slouches on the bunk, takes the locket out, begins to rub it between his thumb and forefinger, as if willing a genie to appear. He says to Senchak, relaxing back into his native Ukrainian, "Germans. Why must we be with them?"

"Sure, just want to work," Senchak says, shrugging. "More time we stopping work, trouble comes. We are here, is all. Yesterday nothing. Tomorrow nothing. Put your hands to work, time goes."

"We fight. Must prove we fight, for Canada. We forget that, here? Must we not fight, also?"

"Better to work, is all."

Petriv stands, takes off his vest and boots, folds himself under the oily wool blanket. Senchak, seeing his words have made no impression, sits where the German did on the bunk's edge, places a hand on Petriv's shoulder. Petriv startles up, eyes wild. Senchak says softly, "*Easy* Petriv. We are here, is all. Yesterday nothing. Tomorrow nothing. But we here. Germans here. Is all. No make trouble. Put your hands to work, is better."

Petriv closes his eyes, content to let Senchak stay. His eyelids are blue-veined and oddly transparent, his pupils like shadows beneath them, as if his eyelids are faulty, worn thin. Maybe some defect from birth. Senchak, unsettled, lifts his hand, passes it across Petriv's eyes, as if he must do the work of eyelids. Senchak considers sliding his other hand beneath the blanket to steal a look inside Petriv's locket. Instead, he goes to the bunkhouse door, cracks it open.

The sentry there, the guard named Brod, lifts his rifle and lets it balance on his gloved hands, as if he doesn't notice the Ukrainian in the doorway. Senchak watches the trees beyond the barbed-wire fence and whirls of thin snow coming down like a further net thrown over the enclosure. Someone yells for him to close the door. He slips a cigarette from the pocket of his jacket, finds matches, strikes one on the back of his corded hand, lets it singe his fingers. Offers the cigarette to Brod, who continues chewing the frosted fray of his handlebar moustache. When Senchak has sucked the cigarette down to a stub, Brod takes a step towards him and, laying the rifle against his leg again, motions for the Ukrainian to go back inside. Senchak drops the cigarette into the new layer of snow, looks at the guard. Brod shrugs and says, "Cold gonna break. Best rest while you can."

Senchak goes in. Petriv is still on his bunk, on his back with blankets twisted around his legs, arms crossed on his chest like a dead man. *Better dead than like child.* The locket chain is wrapped around his inside hand, a blood shadow where the metal presses flesh. Senchak has to lean close to see his eyes are shut. He turns towards the Germans, who talk in their sharp fast way in words he can't understand. Other men laugh and pitch dice against the wall. One man, a Romanian who didn't go with the others, lies on his bunk face down, knees pulled in and buttocks in the air, as if he's mirroring, mocking, the sulphurous mountain that looms over the camp. Senchak feels the impulse to kick him. He goes back outside.

Leans against the wall by the door. Near, the guard Brod talks to the guard Window, who has come down from where the Romanians work. The difference in the sizes of the two guards makes Senchak smile. Window's rifle in his hands is like a child's toy. Senchak turns out of the wind, makes a game of his own breathing, sees faces in his exhalations, like the games with clouds he played as a child in Galicia. Sometimes, the shape of his hot breath comes to resemble a face he remembers. But each melts away, and Senchak is glad.

4

Calgary, Alberta, 2008

WE RENT A CAR AT THE AIRPORT, DRIVE TO THE CITY, CHECK into our hotel. The idea is to get acclimatized, to rest, for our trip into the mountains. I was sure the flight, the rigamarole of travel, would exhaust Dad, but I'm exhausted. I'm here to support him, but all I want is sleep. The car is a black PT Cruiser. It is elegant, stately, "Like a limousine," I say. Dad says, "Like a hearse." The hotel is a Best Western. Dad insisted on it, "Please, no faggoty bed-and-breakfast." But it's seen better days. When we unlock our room, the two double beds are unmade, pillows propped against the headboards, and plastic cups are strewn about on the flesh-coloured rug, each still sealed in its little cellophane bag. One of the chairs is upside down. Dad, on entering, says, "When is something gonna go right on this trip?" Before I can remind him that he chose this hotel, and that things, so far, have gone smoothly (or so I think; in a couple of months, I'll receive a $300 charge from the car rental company, for two speeding tickets from red-light cameras) he makes for the bathroom, shuffling pigeon-toed, says, "I can't wait, better be a toilet roll or I'll use one of their towels, if any are clean."

When I come back with our new room assignment, Dad is sitting in the hall on his hard moulded luggage, wrinkled pant legs splayed out. He looks homeless. He hacks into a handkerchief, examines it then slips it into the front pocket of his shirt, where it'll cosy up to the bitten cookie.

"You all right? You don't look so good." I don't wait for him to answer, say, "They apologized, gave us a luxury room."

Dad jabs his thumb, strange and wizened as a snake's head, towards the offending room, "Big clump of hair in the bathtub drain. Socks and half a hairy candy bar under the bed."

I don't ask why he thoroughly examined the room before abandoning it. May as well ask why water is wet, why wind is windy. "They're sending someone to clean it, pronto, anyway."

"Signs of the former tenant. Take a fumigation, that will," he says.

I try to nap in our newly appointed space. But while I'm sprawled on my bed, feet crossed at the ankles, Dad buzzes around, spreads paper on his own bed, places a beat-up old shoebox, lid secured with a black shoelace, on the table by the window. Through half-closed eyes, lids flickering with irritation—when I squint I look *exactly* like him—I see, like little light flashes, the tumult of his knobby white shoulders and elbows and knees, all the creaky gears of his body working. The papers are ones that he printed from the Internet, information about the World War One internment camps in the National Parks. He studied them on the plane, tried to get me to read them, leaning close and smelling distinctly and sadly like an old man, repeating, *This is your granddad we're talking about* as I stared at the rows of black lines, the words floating and blurring. Now he has them spread out in the hotel room, white squares on the bed, the floor, the small dresser, my legs. I can't sleep, abandon the hope, can hear him shuffling papers, cursing and coughing, realize this trip will be a series of abandonments, life on the road with Dad. But I won't give up easily.

"Dad, please rest. You've looked at this stuff a hundred times. What are you looking for?"

"Can't place Tato with all this stuff. Doesn't seem real."

I push myself into a sitting position against the padded headboard. "Ancient history," I say, embarrassed at the cliché. But something has occurred to Dad, and he begins to arrange the papers into new piles. He sits down in one of the chairs by the wood-veneer table, puts his dry, papery hands on the shoebox, winds the loose shoelace around his fingers. "What's in the box?" I ask, feeling like a straight man. We're some vaguely pathetic comedy duo. "Oh, just ancient history," he says. I'm his punchline. I close my eyes, try to forget the broken skin of information around us, and wish he'd do the same. But Dad never lets anything go.

5

Banff Internment Camp, Cave and Basin, 1916

THE TEMPERATURE BREAKS, AS THE GUARD BROD PREDICTED. After the morning roll call, private Kemper announces that the men will spend the day chopping ice blocks from the river, some of which will be used by local businesses to stock their iceboxes for summer, some for an ice palace for the Banff Winter Carnival, just days away. A wagon waits beyond the enclosure, filled with bales of hay, sawdust, two-man crosscut saws, and shovels and axes and iron pincers for the work. The big brown horse sneezes and stamps. An icy fog shrouds the rugs of its hooves, clings round its mane. Before the men move out, Window approaches Senchak. The Irish guard, wind-cooked and expansive as an oak, deep grooves in his cheeks under each green, blistering eye, speaks to the prisoner in a deferring tone.

"Mr. Senchak. Need your help. Man inside, Kuza, won't work."

"Maybe Kuza sick."

"You speak with him."

"Not Bulgarian," Senchak says.

"No matter. You come. You work hard, harder than most. Men know. He'll see you, understand. Or perhaps you and your men surrender your bunks by the wood stove?" Window grins at Senchak, then turns and walks towards the bunkhouse. The issue has been decided.

Senchak follows. Petriv, at the back of the line, breaks off and follows, is stopped by Ramsay. Senchak hears, turns. Petriv, as if about to give something to the guard, slides a hand inside his jacket, then, looking past him, raises it towards Senchak. The locket dangles from his fingers. Senchak has no idea what this means, what Petriv is trying to do. The moment passes, and Petriv, before Ramsay has to prod him with the bayonet, tucks his locket away, rejoins the line.

Inside the bunkhouse, Window approaches the Bulgarian. Senchak stands back, awaiting instructions. Window, rifle at his side, leans over the form hidden by the blanket, says, "Private Ramsay says you're not inspired to help us today."

The Bulgarian unwinds from the blanket, sits on the edge of the bunk, his shirt lopsided, pants bunched up above his stocking feet. He blanches at the sight of the towering figure, recovers his look of resignation. Says, "Prisoners of war no work. No combatants. You are bound on our *in-car-cer-a-tion*. Nothing more. Kessler says they no work in Vernon. Why we work here?"

Window says, "Can't argue that. You know what's what. But merchants need help, with all the town men gone. Fighting. Dying. *Canadian* men. Maybe you see in your heart."

"Canadian also," Kuza says.

Senchak waits, expects that Window will call on him. Feels a tingling in his arms and shoulders, sudden ache that isn't desire for work. Is relieved that Window doesn't acknowledge him, seems to have forgotten he is there.

Kuza, short but stocky with heavy-lidded eyes and a V-shaped gap in his lower front teeth, doesn't speak again, puts his hands on the wooden lip of his bunk. Window, nodding as if acknowledging the truth of Kuza's words, lifts his rifle, rests its bayonet with its blood gutter on his own shoulder, drops the butt end towards the seated Bulgarian, as if offering it to him. Kuza, confused, doesn't move, then rests his hands on the rifle, which Window has positioned so the butt rests against the inside of Kuza's thigh.

Window leans on the rifle, lightly at first, the hub of his large hand against the barrel. Kuza pushes back but is no match for the guard. He twists like a pinned insect—his feet lift, knuckles burn white, and a long string of spit shivers from the gap in his teeth. He doesn't cry out, but Senchak sees the skull inside his face. Window eases the gun off. Kuza drops to the floor, coughs, blurts out, as if the words are hot tears he is loath to release, "*Kuchi sin*, you pay for this." He tugs at his pant legs, covers the pale flesh of his ankles, as if they are the source of his pain, embarrassment.

"We make mistake sometime," Window says, resting his rifle at his side, at ease. "I am no guard, you no prisoner. Just between us, this. Between men. Bulgarian, Austrian. No matter. We work. You misunderstand is all. Mr. Senchak saw us talk. Now, talk is done."

Window reaches inside his greatcoat, finds a cigarette, offers it to Kuza who, without looking, waves it away. Window clicks his heels, salutes the Bulgarian with a sincere snap of his wrist, motions for Senchak to follow.

The other men have moved and follow the horse and wagon through hard icy ruts towards the river. Window stands silent with the other guard who waits to inspect the bunkhouse, even as Kuza appears in the doorway, collar around his face, his boots on the wrong feet. He moves by them, joins the line of men. Stops, steps out from the group, pulls his boots off, stands for too long in the snow in his stocking feet before pulling his boots on again, correctly. None of the men watch him accomplish this.

6

Calgary, Alberta, 2008

MY FATHER SLEEPS FITFULLY. HIS SLEEP IS A WRESTLING MATCH of flips, curls, stretches, recoils, of blubbering moans and choking yawns, of rattles and liquid hacks, all interrupted by trips to the bathroom, almost every hour. I worry about his prostate, a man his age. Sometimes I forget how old my dad is. I feel as though, sleeping near him, I've bedded down in a forest, close to where two night creatures are in dispute or in anguished lust, turning over one another like rapids in a river. It occurs to me that, with Dad in close proximity, I don't really need to visit the wilderness—his body is predator and prey rolled into one animal hunting, feeding on itself. When morning comes, my father appears well rested, but I'm beaten, hollowed out, as if I'm the bed he slept on. I have the sense that his style of sleep is meant to annoy me, an argument against me. I'm not entirely sure what we're arguing about.

7

Banff Internment Camp, Cave and Basin, 1916

THAT NIGHT, AFTER THE MEN HAVE RETURNED FROM THE RIVER, sweaty beneath their clothes but chilled, bitten on their extremities, there is another incident in the bunkhouse. Senchak has stepped outside for a cigarette—he makes a game of how he draws on it, sucks in his cheeks, with a flourish plucks it from his mouth, blows a rope of smoke into darkness—when he hears a commotion. Despite his proximity to the door, the camp guards Ramsay and Kemper arrive before him.

Inside, in the stuttering light, the Germans have formed a hard circle, outside of which the other men push, climb onto bunks or one another for a view. One of the Romanians tears a cross-slat of wood from a bunk. Another bangs a tin canteen on the floor. Ramsay and Kemper, with their glinting bayonets, split the crowd. At the centre, near the roaring wood stove, two of the Germans hold Petriv. They lift him towards the hot iron, attempt to press his face against it. On the guards' arrival, the Germans let him drop, but he scrambles back and claws at the one who'd been steering him: Kessler. In a flash, the guards have pulled their rifles against the throats of the two grappling men, drag them away from one another. Window arrives, takes a place by the wood stove. The guards force Kessler and Petriv down the aisle between bunks. Senchak waits in the shadows.

Window stays. In the baleful half-light, he resembles some kind of ogre or storybook giant ready to devour or disembowel the remaining men. Grins with a gargoyle look that reminds the men that he'd enjoy nothing so much as returning in the night to punish them for disturbing his sleep. After a time, and with a menacing backward glance, he goes out into the cold and snow and saunters among the low stars.

The Romanians resume a card game. The Bulgarians, closer to the Germans, gather around one of their own, a man with permanently raised eyebrows and a cleft chin, who has drawn some large, loopy cartoon figures on the wall above his bunk: caricatures of German officers with spiked helmets and donkey tails, trampling over stick-like soldiers with xs for eyes. Kuza laughs louder than the rest, stops when he sees the men staring. Senchak, at first, sits on his bunk by the wood stove close to the other Ukrainians, shrugging his shoulders, trying to loosen the knots. When he stands and approaches the Romanians, the small circle opens, the men sliding back against their bunks, playing cards fanning from their hands. Senchak addresses the Romanian who stands to face him, a man named Krisman. Senchak asks him what caused the incident.

"Petriv near Germans. Talking. He shouts, throws blanket over one. Others get him, try cook his face. We make ice castle tomorrow, no?"

"Tomorrow," says Senchak.

"Tomorrow, better than today."

Senchak considers. "Today today. Tomorrow tomorrow. Yesterday, tomorrow, not-ting."

The Romanian looks at him. Smiles and raises his playing cards to tell the Ukrainian that their conversation is done.

THE PRISONERS MARCH TOWARDS THE BANFF TOWNSITE, behind the horse and cart. It's weighed down by large squares of ice, each one separated from the next by a rug of hay. Senchak marches a few bodies back from Petriv, but notes the younger man's pronounced limp and how he favours his right arm. He appears headless, his coat pulled up on his shoulders, face pushed down against the bone buttons. Both Petriv and his adversary, Kessler, have joined the group after emerging from the guards' bunkhouse, where they spent the night under close watch. But Window has placed Kessler in the line directly behind Petriv. A decision has been made that requires that the two men endure proximity. When another of the Germans breaks from his place to approach Kessler, Window forces him back.

As the men parade across the Bow River bridge, the structure complaining, a crosswind rises. The prisoners lower their heads. The guards do the same, but owing to the rifles propped against their necks, bayonets high, they maintain a regal stance. Some children appear, their faces red and eyes shining beneath woolen caps. They follow alongside the prisoners, veering close then spinning off, appearing to taunt the prisoners with their freedom, then hiding behind their mothers and fathers, who stand in two small groups off the road by the first buildings. The women, in their long coats, wide-brimmed hats, and with fringed parasols open against the falling snow, resemble the winter trees that enclose the camp barracks. The men smoke. As the prisoners draw close, the women half turn towards the ragged line, while the smokers break up and form a semi-circle around them. Laughter. Among them, Ukrainian faces: Senchak recognizes the high cheekbones, steep foreheads, the almond eyes. He doesn't allow himself to consider why he is imprisoned and these others walk free, indeed are tourists in this new mountain park. He is here because he couldn't find work in Edmonton then, unaware of the restriction, journeyed to the American border. But these others, these husbands and wives, mothers and fathers, might return to sleep in the rich vaulted rooms of the Banff Hotel, and he to a poor narrow bunk. Thinking these thoughts, he grows displeased, relaxes when he concentrates on the work at hand.

The men begin to unload the ice blocks from the wagon. The horse is so still that Senchak thinks it has died on its feet. He considers how he'd prefer such a death. But its nostrils blast steam, and fresh cannonballs tumble from its rear. One of the men walks between the horse and wagon, warms his hands over the steaming pile before Window prods him back. The master of the winter carnival, a small, weasel-faced man named Nevens, directs the prisoners, as two at a time heft the heavy ice blocks into rows on the street. Senchak sees that Petriv and Kessler have neared the front, will have to work together to remove an ice block. He also sees that the German has a new bruise below his left eye that joins the stain on his chin and neck. This is evidence, along with Petriv's limp, that the guards spent part of the night persuading these men not to cause any more problems.

When they arrive at the wagon, the two prisoners lock eyes. As the ice block is lowered, Petriv and Kessler take either end of it. They shuffle it over to the place that forms the first tier of the ice palace. Kessler, once they've dropped the load, nods at Petriv, and the two men retreat. Window joins them. The giant has several burning cigarettes wedged between the shaft of his rifle and the attached bayonet. It appears his rifle is alive, exhaling into the frigid air. He ushers Petriv and Kessler out of the line, away from the other prisoners, and plucks one then another of the cigarettes from his rifle. For a few moments, as the work continues, Petriv and Kessler and Window stand together, smoking.

At the same time, the Bulgarian Kuza is slow to secure his side of an ice block. Unable to support the full weight, his partner, a Ukrainian named Boyko, stumbles, tries to heave the block off to the side, falls hard on the frozen street. The other men laugh. The fallen man comes up with torn elbows, blood mingling in strings with the strands of his sleeves. He curses Kuza, who approaches and tries to put a calming hand on his arm. Boyko pulls away, spits a curse. Then turns and embraces Kuza. The bear hug is both violent and forgiving.

The work resumes, but the men are distracted by the small crowd that formed when the Ukrainian hit the street, the same women, men, and children who appeared at the edge of town. An automobile pulls up just short of the wagon, rasping in the cold. Inside are three men in black hats and thick fur collars, and one flat-nosed, blonde-haired woman, a fox biting its tail around her neck. From the car's rumble seat extend the wooden slats of skis. The automobile swings around the horse and wagon and stops in front of the Natural History Museum, an old building whose leaky roof the prisoners helped repair when they first arrived at the camp. The passengers go inside to look at the stuffed animals in glass curio cabinets: the wolves, mountain lions and bears, the snarling but glass-eyed specimens that represent the fauna of the surrounding wilderness.

Before long, the ice palace takes shape, with an ice-block entrance which leads to a crude maze, the body of the structure. As the building nears completion, two of the prisoners wander into it, are followed by Window. Outside, some of the remaining men explode into laughter when they realize they can still see the big Irishman, his head clearing the incomplete walls. He soon dances the men out of the maze with his bayonet. Before he emerges, he stops, lays his chin on the uppermost block of ice near the entrance, grins and leers at the crowd. The other guards point, hoot and holler. The prisoners fall silent, unwilling to share the moment with their captors. When Window tries to lift his chin, it sticks, stretches. He leaves a patch of skin and blood.

As they all march back through the dusk, alpenglow, burning red, plays on the mountain above the town. Petriv keeps turning, slowing, to watch the changing, sliding light. He soon stops altogether, leans forward on his toes, eyes bulging towards where the sun pauses. He closes and opens them, taking the view in little visual sips. While the rest of the men move on, Petriv remains, but isn't alone. Window waits. Senchak drops back too, lets the line of men shuffle past. After a few moments, Window steps in front of Petriv, blocks his view, tells him to keep moving. Petriv stares up, mesmerized, and Senchak, too, sees that alpenglow touches the giant's skull. Even the sun mistakes Window for a mountain. Senchak blinks the image away just as Petriv recoils, limps back towards him. Petriv takes the locket out from the pouch he's sewn inside his vest, sees that Window watches. Drops his head, makes a tent of his coat, but keeps his feet moving. Senchak places a firm hand between his shoulder blades, guides him in the right direction.

8

Calgary, Alberta, 2008

WE REJECT THE CRUMBLING DONUTS AND THIN COFFEE offered in the hotel lobby, the elegant sounding "Continental

Breakfast." We stop at a Tim Hortons on the outskirts of town. Next stop, the mountains and the new monument that is the reason for our visit.

We avoid the drive-through, several cars making a figure eight in the parking lot, and join the line on the inside. I tell Dad he can find us seats while I wait to get our English muffins, but he doesn't. He's perturbed by the long line, so needs to exercise his annoyance, to take it for a walk like a small dog. He's mostly perturbed, I soon see, by the sight of the only person taking orders, an older South Asian lady. She's clearly distressed and requires help, but her colleagues are all occupied: two giraffe-like blonde teenage boys bobbing and weaving behind the soup/sandwich counter, and a gaggle of girls administering to the drive-through traffic, radio headsets fastened to their ears. I suggest to Dad that we'd be better off going through the drive-through, but he gives me a look as if I've asked him to cut off his right hand.

We wait. Dad keeps stepping in and out of line, peering above the crowd. He bites, chews, his lower lip. The woman is doing her best. Her hands move quickly with the coffee cups. Strings of coffee arc through the air. There's coffee between her fingers and coffee on her arms. Her black hair, tied in a bun below her green Tim Hortons visor, has shaken loose, she keeps blowing a strand of it from her eyes. Once or twice, the poor woman, confused by the onslaught of requests, *Double-cream no sugar, one cream three sugar, double-double, double-milk one sugar, one decaf black, a maple dip not maple cream donut, an old-fashioned plain donut, not a glazed old-fashioned plain donut with vanilla sprinkles*, sets both her hands on the counter and closes her eyes. The lineup of customers grows and surges.

Dad makes a nocturnal sound and steps, figuratively and literally, out of line. I shrink. He shouts, "Can't anyone help this poor woman? What kind of place you running here?" The whole place pauses. Heads pivot, patrons at tables in mid-sentence mid-bite and mid-sip, coffee cups or iPhones at the ends of their arms. Things resume. The coffee machine begins again. I see a commotion through the door behind the counter, and a young woman, not in the standard Tim Hortons uniform, but in a black halter top, with a bracelet-of-thorns tattoo circling her right arm—she looks vaguely Goth, wholly angry—comes out and punches open a second cash register, narrows her crow eyes as if daring anyone to approach.

When we reach the counter, the South Asian lady doesn't acknowledge my father. He winks at her and says, "Hope they start treating you better dear. Ridiculous what they expect." She smiles, she deals with loony men all the time, looks past him and says, "Seven-ninety please."

Once we're sitting, he starts in.

"Disgraceful. Immigrants forced to take these jobs. Part-time, you can bet, then they don't have to pay benefits. We shouldn't patronize these people."

"She seems to be handling it all right."

"It's in the job description. You can't frown at Timmy Hortons."

I study the other employees. There are some smiles, but they aren't standard issue. Even the Goth girl is joking with a customer now. I don't say anything. But as I sip my coffee, purse my lips around the white mug's rim, my whole life suddenly feels as pursed, tentative, painful, and particular as the way I'm drinking. I wish I'd spoken up like my dad did.

Before we leave, a middle-aged man, around my age, in crisp new jeans and scuffed silver cowboy boots, long greying hair in a ponytail, stops by our table and says to my dad,

"Thanks for saying something. Place makes money hand over fist. Canada's Goldman Sachs."

Dad barely responds, just whispers, "You bet," without looking up. The man waits for a more meaningful interaction. I say, "Thanks." He nods and moves off. His cowboy boots snap along the sticky floor.

9

Banff Internment Camp, Cave and Basin, 1917

JANUARY 6TH. THE UKRAINIANS GATHER TO CELEBRATE *Sviatyi Vechir*, Holy Eve. They shift some of the bunks so they can come together by the wood stove at the western end of the bunkhouse. One of the older men, a slight but whip-strong Ukrainian named Chaban, has stolen hay from the wagon outside, and has set up, in a close corner, a *Didukh*, the hay formed into a sheaf. The man also produces, to the amazement of the others, a small loaf of bread. "Window is our friend," he laughs. Next, he slides, like a magician, a burning candle from inside his sleeve, with a flourish twists it into the loaf, approximating the look of a *Kalach*, the traditional bread. A skinny brown bottle appears, is passed from hand to hand. Shouts of surprise and pleasure, though some of the men refuse to drink, alcohol forbidden on this eve. But all the men feel expansive, as if their celebratory proximity creates a new energy, a collective soul that streams out and blunts the sharp cold night, sure as the smoke and heat from the wood stove.

In search of something else, none of the men can understand what it is, Petriv breaks from the group and moves towards the Germans who, as usual, are seated by the eastern wood stove, engaged in their own conversation. Petriv takes his locket out and begins, in the midst of them, to swing it pendulum style in front of his own face. His eyes bulge. Next, he crouches and swings it close to the wood stove, as if cooking the contents. Repeats, "Good Christmas, good Christmas vee having." None of the Germans reacts. After several minutes, Kessler, not moving from the edge of his bunk, says, "Why doing this? Game? Then give us look what is inside." Petriv doesn't respond and keeps the locket swinging. Kessler rises, steps towards him.

Senchak watches, approaches down the main aisle. Sees that Kessler is genuinely disturbed by the locket, as if there is some witchcraft in its movement, that its repetitive swinging echoes or foretells the dull repetition of their lives, each of their days, weeks, months, the same, the same, and again the same. As if the swinging, glinting locket is some obscure but ominous part of the Ukrainian celebration, a curse upon those who do not share their tradition.

Kessler is unnerved. He asks Petriv to put his jewellery away, to go back to his Christmas. Crouches next to him. The German begins to speak again, but there is a difference in his tone, a tremor of intent: "I giving you Christmas gift."

He comes up with a blade, a thin piece of sharp hammered metal he's pulled from inside his boot. Senchak flies from the shadows, twists Kessler's arm behind him, spraining it, numbing it. The blade drops. The other Germans close in, but hesitate when they see Senchak's eyes rolling back in his head.

Senchak releases the German, takes Petriv instead, shouts, "Fool, stick you myself." As Senchak hoists him by his shirt and trousers, Petriv manages, almost calmly, to wrap the locket and chain around his hand again. Senchak deposits him on his bunk, watches as he curls up, locket wrapped around his hand at the centre of him now.

Soon after, Chaban decides, under the circumstances, and acting the magician again, to break the tradition he tried to preserve: he removes the dripping candle from the bread loaf, twists it, still burning, into the bunkhouse wall. Cracks the waxy loaf with his long fingers, passes crumbling pieces to his countrymen and to the other men who are still standing, watching the Germans. He goes to offer some to them, too, but turns back; they are closed, impervious, gathered around Kessler in conference. Near them, something thumps heavily against the bunkhouse wall, as if a large animal has lost its way, made mad by the cold and darkness. After, the men ponder what has and hasn't happened, resign themselves, even on this night, to another troubled fall towards sleep.

LATER, WHILE THE OTHER MEN SLEEP, SENCHAK DRESSES, tries to go outside, but the door is barred. Hearing him, the night sentry, a new man named Morris, lifts the crossbeam and opens the door, nervous but happy for the diversion. He steps back but keeps his rifle propped against his shoulder. He says, "You have a problem inside?"

Senchak steps from the doorway, unlit cigarette in his mouth. Shakes his coat to find matches, lights the cigarette, offers it. Morris waves it away, drops his rifle to his side. Senchak sucks on the cigarette, nods in return, says, with no expression, as if the cold with its razor edge has shaved off everything extraneous, "You hear animals?"

Morris says, "What? Hear animals? Coyotes, you mean? Probably too cold even for them."

Senchak says, "Listen. Vee hear animals. Wolf. Coyote. Bear, also. But not howling. Dey talk. Dey talk, like you and me."

The guard tilts his head, waits for an explanation.

Senchak continues, "Holy Night, animals talk. I go listen."

Morris laughs, says, "What, wolves and coyotes and deer

sit down together, have conversation? Maybe. But you ain't joinin' them."

Both men stand in the close and holy darkness, watch the outline of the trees, the moonlight on the snow. They listen and listen. Morris doesn't know the prisoner, but, despite the man's wide shoulders, windburnt face, and severe black eyes, relaxes in his presence.

Senchak flicks his cigarette away and says to the guard, "Tank you. *Khrystos rodyvsia*. Vee heard animals for sure." He goes back inside.

Senchak sits on his bunk, watches Petriv. In the firelight, Petriv's locket rises and falls on his chest, chain wrapped loosely around his hand. Strange for him to leave his locket exposed. Senchak has the sense that the locket is an eye—a third eye for Petriv. Thinks of Petriv's damaged eyelids. The locket blinks. Blinks again. Disturbed, Senchak removes his boots and jacket, climbs onto his own bunk on top of the blanket. Faces away from Petriv, tries to ignore, to forget, *Full hopeless*, Petriv's third, scorching eye.

10

Calgary and Banff, Alberta, 2008

BEFORE WE GET BACK ON THE ROAD, THE TWO-HOUR DRIVE to the mountains, Dad asks to retrieve his bag from the trunk. He soon has the familiar papers spread out on his thighs in the passenger seat, the shoebox between his feet. The back seat is empty, but he likes to have everything close around him.

"Dad, why don't you enjoy the scenery? What are you looking for?" I can't stop needling him. And even though I want him to appreciate the immediate landscape, there's comfort in our futile banter. Before long, I'll likely be obsessing over the past too, cradling old shoeboxes as if they're treasure chests.

"Not looking for anything. Reminding myself of the facts, getting the facts straight before we arrive."

I don't say anything. I know he'll continue without my prodding, his words, now, as insistent as the foothills piling up beyond the windows.

"The government had no right. Encouraged to settle here, then betrayed. Far from family. Nobody screams loud enough. We need to keep making noise."

"Wasn't Granddad alone? Didn't he meet Grandma much later?"

"He lost three years. He was angry. He never had time for *our* complaints. Wouldn't come back here, after that. Don't blame him."

"Grandma didn't care for the mountains. Said she was an ocean girl."

"When she say that?"

"She ran things. I remember how quiet Granddad was. She did all the talking."

"He drank. Those days, nobody said *alcoholic*. You don't know. Spent most his time at that Ukrainian place on Mission Street. Came home drunk most nights."

"He didn't seem angry."

"You don't know. There were things he wouldn't talk about."

"Maybe he talked to Grandma. What does your sister say?"

"Don't care what Emily says."

"Grandma seemed happy."

"Looks are deceiving."

"Grandma wasn't happy?"

"Far as it goes."

"She had that crazy laugh, she'd get us all laughing."

"You can't imagine what she put up with."

"Dad, you're too sensitive. Mom used to say. He was only in that camp for three years. Wasn't a life sentence."

"You can bet his cancer had something to do with it."

"Lots of men get prostate cancer. He lived till, what, eighty-five? Hope I last that long. They seemed happy. If he wasn't put in that camp, he probably wouldn't have moved east, met Grandma. You wouldn't have been born. Or maybe he would have gone back to Ukraine before he met her. Why didn't he go back, if he was so angry?"

"Wasn't Ukraine at the time."

"He chose to stay. Canada was a blessing, even after everything."

He goes back to his pages, rifles through them as if he's misplaced some vital piece of information, some key. Feeling his agitation, I'm reminded of a Ukrainian folktale I learned as a child. Can't remember all the details. It was about two young sisters who, worked mercilessly on the farm by their widower father, make a suicide pact, then braid their long wheat-coloured hair together and jump into the river. I imagine that my father and his father have done something similar, sadness winding them together, although separated by years and circumstance. The work of binding the living to the dead. Also, Dad and me. This is what this trip is doing, whether I like it or not. And perhaps I'm bound to him by this flourish, my increasing need for meaning, for drama. Why did I agree to join him on this journey, knowing him like I do?

11

Banff Internment Camp, Cave and Basin, 1917

A HOWL CRACKS THE MORNING AIR. A HOWL THAT GOES UP IN the bunkhouse, shakes dust from the rafters, sends bats skittering along inside the roof. The men start from their dreams. Sound becomes an awful yelping, like the noises the men hear nightly when coyotes gather around a kill. It is Petriv. Senchak wakes to hear him, the words mostly incoherent, "You have, you *have*, kill, kill you."

Petriv, near naked, scrambles from his bed. He flies above the rows of bunks. Before Senchak arrives, three of the Germans wrestle Petriv to the floor, press his pale shoulders and hips into the rough floorboards. Kessler, the target of his attack, escapes his grasp, backs up against the wall by the wood stove. In loose pants and torn shirt, he breathes rapidly, launches clouds into the air, touches his own neck in a demure way, and watches the pinned, writhing figure. This time, Senchak stands back, watches too.

After Petriv's removal, the men gather around the eastern wood stove. Kuza explains how he watched Petriv searching his bunk, next his own clothes, stripping them off, pulling them inside out. Kessler, listening, crosses his arms and waits, tries for an ease that will make the men forget the fear he couldn't hide, "No have his jewellery. Dummkopf is crazy. Now, we win maybe some peace."

Petriv is moved into the guardhouse, until he can be transferred to another internment camp, or given a supervised job at one of the local logging companies until the war's end. When Senchak asks for details, Ramsay tells him that, for the safety of the guards, Petriv, at night, will be chained to his bunk in the guardhouse. Senchak offers to keep a closer watch on his friend. He is willing to have them chained together, if necessary. Ramsay laughs and says, "Right, like Si-a-mese twins, sure. It's out of my hands."

The next morning, as the men rise from their bunks, they hear shouting from outside, find the bunkhouse door barred against them. They gather at a window, through swirls of frost watch men with leather bags arrive at the guardhouse. Some of the prisoners recognize them as workers from the infirmary. Next, a big man on horseback. Kuza thinks it's Major Cruikshank, the camp commander, though none of the men can say for sure. Window, among the men outside, notices the prisoners at the window, faces stacked in a sad totem. He plucks the crossbeam from the bunkhouse door, goes inside and announces that roll call is delayed. There's been an accident. He's vague and distracted, but lets his gaze rest for too long on Senchak, who, a tingling in his hands, turns away.

12

Banff, Alberta, 2008

WE ARRIVE. A SIGN DIRECTS US FROM THE BOW VALLEY Parkway. As we pull off the road towards Castle Mountain, Dad says, "Prisoners built these roads. You know Dad helped build the Banff golf course? Think they ever invited him back to play a round?"

"Mountain does look like a castle."

Dad doesn't look up but strains forward, lifts the shoebox.

The monument is close to the road, in amongst the sweet-smelling trees. It has two parts, the main one the bronze statue of a short mustached man in a hat and overalls, his right hand extended, palm upward. To the statue's right is a plaque bolted to a slab of stone that explains the context, a fresh bouquet of pink carnations propped against it. Someone else has visited today.

While I look around, Dad stays in the car, still working to untie the lace from the shoebox. Groans as he climbs out. Says as he approaches, "This was the summer camp. In winter, the Cave and Basin. This is the only place, far as I know, where there's a monument."

I'm not really listening, but not because I've heard it before. Seeing my dad struggle, and hearing the weariness in his voice, is hard. I should have helped him out of the car, should stand with him as he studies the monument. But my compassion is third hand. Dad is closer in time to the events commemorated here. I drop back, let him have a private moment in remembrance of his father, his *Tato*.

He is silent for a long time. The irritation that usually cramps his face is gone. Then, he approaches the statue, puts one of his hands on the bronze knee, hangs his head. I say, "Are you okay? What are you doing?" He turns and shows me the thing he's taken from the shoebox, something I've never seen before—a silver locket on a chain. "Won't be able to manage it," he says. "Could you put this around the statue's neck? You'll have to tie it, the chain's broke." The locket swings as he lowers it into my hands, the tarnished oval landing first, the tiny chain pooling on top. It's surprisingly heavy for such a small thing.

13

Banff Internment Camp, Cave and Basin, 1917

THE MEN CLEAR DEEP FRESH SNOW FROM THE BANFF ROAD. They scoop a thin trench, a valley within the valley. Senchak approaches Window, keeps his shovel up, letting the guard know he only means to pause from work to ask: *What exact happened in guardhouse, and where right now is Petriv?*

Window takes the new cigarette that burns near his rifle's bayonet, draws on it. Offers it to Senchak, who shakes his head then watches Window condemn it to whiteness. When Window speaks, his voice is small. Senchak has to lean in.

"In the morning, Petriv's bunk empty. Believe he escaped. But chains still there. Blood. He's curled underneath, like child, blade still in hand. He'd cut his own throat. Sorry, Mr. Senchak. Sorry we must play this game in this place."

Senchak resumes. The road is just a narrow stagger, an animal pathway through the snow. The men around him are half-men, only their torsos visible. They bend, straighten, heave the dead weight over their shoulders, to the sides. Quickly, Senchak—steam rising from him, as if he's a thermal spring, another Cave and Basin—has cleared the whole area around him down to hard ringing ground. The other men stare. They've barely made a dent in the implacable whiteness, in the weight that won't yield, in the winter that won't end.

Senchak works into darkness. The new guards, the men assigned to replace Ramsay and Morris—suspended until further investigation into the Petriv incident—order him to stop, to return with the others. They aim their bayonets in a kind of sad embarrassment. The next morning, at roll call, Senchak emerges from the bunkhouse fully dressed before the other men have climbed from their bunks.

14

Banff, Alberta, 2008

I STAND THERE, THE LOCKET IN MY HANDS. DON'T WANT to unfasten the little clasp and look inside without Dad's permission. I say, "What is this? I assume it's Granddad's?"

He goes and crouches beside the stone with the inscription. "He kept that box from those camp years. Not much in it. Old pair of mittens, a torn piece of fabric. And that locket."

I turn the locket over. It's tarnished and scratched. Anticipating Dad's surliness, but also a little hurt, I say, "What's inside? Why didn't you tell me about this?"

Not taking the bait, he says, "Take a look. The lock is tricky, though."

I manage to unhook the clasp, tiny hammer wedged inside a metal ring. Open it. Wisps of light-coloured hair, most tiny as eyelashes, some longer, curled inside the oval. They've been so long in the locket that they're fused to it, half melted into the metal.

"Whose hair is it?"

"No idea. Got the shoebox a few years back, before Mom died. She gave it to me. I think she was embarrassed. Thought the hair was from another woman. Dad wouldn't say. She assumed it was from the love of his life. Said we all have the love of our lives when we're young. Said it didn't bother her, but I knew she was hurt that he kept it."

"Maybe from some woman back in Ukraine?"

"Maybe. Attend to the locket, will you? I think it's right we leave it here."

We're leaving it. I'm surprised I'm part of the gesture. I close the locket, push the hammer through the loop. Climb up onto the statue, put my arm through the statue's arm. Place the locket around the neck. But can't manage to tie the chain. I go back to the car, steal a paper clip from Dad's sheaf of documents. Bend it into a hook and slide it into one end of the locket chain. Place the locket around the neck again, but drop the paper clip. I can't believe Dad isn't scolding me. I complain, sarcastically, "Oh, why must we suffer." I find the paper clip, manage to fasten the chain around the statue's neck, bend the clip into place, leave the locket hanging there.

I stand before the statue. Dad stays crouched by the stone and inscription. He doesn't examine my handiwork. I worry that his back or knees have given out; he's frozen in commiseration, stiff as the statue. He says, "Supposed to be ruins of the old barracks around here, in the woods. Maybe we can find them. Then we'll visit the Cave and Basin. Want to see what he saw. Maybe we'll play some golf."

"You don't golf," I say. "I don't golf."

He smiles briefly, pushes himself off the bronze plaque, says, "Wish I would have come here with *him*."

"But he *wouldn't* have," I say, trying not to take offence. "And there would have been no monument."

"And no locket. It belongs here, *in honour of George Senchak's memory and all the unnamed prisoners who suffered in these mountains*." He says the words in a formal way, speech he's prepared in advance, but without his curmudgeonly tone, without irony. He turns towards the road. I guess he's decided he doesn't want to rummage through the woods, looking for the past. Seeing the monument and leaving the locket, his father's locket, are enough. We're suddenly aware of the buzz of traffic, the stink of exhaust, cars and trailers passing the monument, passing us. It's busy in these mountains.

As we approach the car, I say, trying to restore some of his combativeness, "Well, our limo awaits." I push back against the sadness that has taken over, sadness that won't leave space for irritation, Dad's prickly need to get everything that's coming to him. I think of the woman on the plane, her annoyance an acknowledgement, a sort of celebration. We need to celebrate. Suggest to Dad that we find a bar, share a strong drink, curse this place, curse these mountains, toast his dead dad. "Damn right," he agrees.

We get back on the road and move fast and faster away from the locket, returned to the mountains with its unknown story.

A NOTE ON THE STORY

During the First World War and in the immediate post-war period (1914–1920) Canadian Internment Operations imprisoned more than 8,000 individuals. The majority of those interned were civilian non-combatants, Ukrainians and other immigrants (Hungarians, Czechs, Slovaks, Croats, Poles, Slovenes) who had come to Canada from the Austro-Hungarian Empire to work in industry or to settle on western homesteads. Twenty-four receiving stations and internment camps were established across Canada.* Although those who ran the camps may have referred to the prisoners in a general way as "Austrians," in the story I've restored their ethnic designations, for the sake of clarity in identifying the different groups that were forced to coexist under trying circumstances.

*Bohdan S. Kordan and Peter Melnycky, eds., *In the Shadow of the Rockies: Diary of the Castle Mountain Internment Camp, 1915–1917*. Edmonton: U of Alberta P, 1991.

Also useful in researching the above material were the books *Enemy Aliens, Prisoners of War: Internment in Canada During the Great War*, by Bohdan S. Kordan; *Without Just Cause, Canada's First National Internment Operations and the Ukrainian Canadians, 1914-1920*, by Lubomyr Y. Luciuk;

The Canadian Rockies, A History in Photographs, by Graeme Pole; *The Stories Were Not Told: Canada's First World War Internment Camps*, by Sandra Semchuk; and *Park Prisoners: The Untold Story of Western Canada's National Parks, 1915–1946*, by Bill Waiser.

GOTH GIRLS OF BANFF

Wanna add some edge to your mountain experience? To sharpen the dull blade of things, and let darkness descend, like beautiful sleep but with your eyes wide open? Call the Goth Girls of Banff. Available for photo shoots, social events, hikes, campfires, singly or in groups. Fully outfitted in deepest and darkest Gothwear, we can be more or less Vampiric, more or less Victorian, more or less Silent Film Man-Eaters and Vamps, and more or less Necromantic and Living Dead, according to special requests. If you're tired of silly Tilley hats and Gore-Tex, cotton and khaki and crave a touch of leather and lace, we're the gory Goth girls dressed up just for you. We're all about Goth aesthetics, no funny business, no sticky situations, no touchy-feely or long longing gazes, and absolutely no fiddly long-term relations. Interactions start at $100 per hour. Prices negotiable for entire afternoons. Can talk evenings for a fee. Request times, locations and nature of encounters. Terms and conditions apply and must be set prior to engagements. Goth Girls of Banff. We'll wrap dark wings around your wilderness day.

SO THIS IS A RECKONING—YEAH, SORT OF A DEAD RECKONING of how and why our Goth life ended. At least, how Linda's Goth career came to end. Linda, my alpha and omega, omega in the ascendant now, but not entirely. After all, she was the one got us started as Goths in the first place, and she was always *the one*, the first and foremost, you'll see. But I didn't think things were so, excuse me, *grave*. We had some good and bad times and Gothic experiences that were naughty and nice. That's life all over, isn't it? Light and dark, sweet and mean: a dog's soft belly or a dog's bum and breakfast. That's how it goes and that's what I think. But Linda always said, pushing her little sister down, "Jessie, leave the thinking to me. Your brain isn't equipped for figuring things out in these dark matters."

When we were on a job, she didn't want me thinking or speaking at all. She didn't want our clients to talk either, to get up close and personal. "It's about mystique," she'd say, spraying me with the word. "Make no mistake. The image is what drives the business, just as the ghost drives the machine." She'd make a spooky-film noise, stick her face close. I wasn't sure what she meant, but grinned anyway.

The last few months had been strange for sure. The first bad experience in those last days, the one that pushed Linda over the edge and round the big bend, as she said, took the shadowy shape of our seventh client that summer (scary number seven, like the seventh seal unsealed in our little lives), a WWII vet named Elmer Spragge. He was sweet as his goofy name, bristly and old as a BC Douglas fir but cute as a pencil. And he looked like a chewed up pencil, forehead scarred below his eraser-hair, with a red thumbprint on the nape of his neck. I guess he'd done the dye job himself. He had the darkest, bruised-blue eyes I'd ever seen, and they matched his Canadian Legion jacket, lapels clotheslined with medals. The weight of them pulled him forward, as if some deathless demon had taken his beef-jerky arm and was hurrying the old soldier along.

He'd seen our ad in the mountain paper *The Bergschrund*. Elmer was intrigued, hired us for an afternoon. When we met him, Linda whispered in my bejewelled ear: "He looks like he'll croak in the middle of the job." I wanted to say, "What a way to go," but didn't. We spent the first fifteen minutes outside the Royal Canadian Legion hall on Banff Avenue, examining Elmer's medals (the only medals I'd ever seen were fake ones, gold wrapped chocolate discs in *Sugar Mountain*). He had ten or so on his scooped-out chest, hanging from a rainbow ribbon. The one he was really proud of was pinned high, separate—a white metal badge, maple-leaf shaped, inset with tiny rhinestones and a number two in the middle. He'd served in the *Queen's Own Rifles*. I tried to get interested, but when I got close, almost nibbling his lapel, he smelled bad, with a ripe, cemetery stink. Where did he live, in a grave, tomb, or crypt, place unsealed so he could seek us out, hoping we were from the same smoking hole? I admit I kind of liked the idea.

We always drew a crowd. We made quite a scene, an irresistible tableau, like a daguerreotype portrait. Or maybe more like a 3-D image from one of those old stereograph viewers: an ancient soldier, frail but spry, and me and Linda flanking him in all our Goth glory—me in a lace corset with a thin minstrel top over it, flared sleeves and black fingerless gloves, she in a medieval gown with a laced-up V-neck front, high slits up the sides, and crosshatched with lace. Linda also wore a crown of thorns made from leather. Both of us with dungeon eyes and bee-sting lips. Regular folk halted on the sidewalk right in the pedestrian traffic flow and gawked, charmed or appalled or both—we were avenging angels come to fly the geezer either up above the bright mountains, or down into one of Satan's sulphur pits.

As he led us inside the Legion hall, Colonel Moore Branch #26, Linda leaned into me, bit my tender ear with, "Don't get the old coot talking. Got a bad feeling about this one. He'll blab about how many men he killed in the war. Just some pics and we're gone. You sit close to him." Hadn't occurred to me that Elmer might have killed men. Now I wanted to hear, and pictured Elmer cracking an eggshell corset, post-battle, looking for comfort and love. Sex and death, what else is there, anyway?

We were in a dimly lit room with a bar at one end and a small mauve couch and a few ratty looking chairs. The walls were gummy panelled wood. There was an alcove with a dartboard nailed to a washroom door, and a hand-scribbled sign suggesting that anyone needing to "use the toilet" should interrupt the game. Two old guys were playing, one of them taking aim, alligator hand moving back and forth in rehearsal, feathers kissing his eye. The other had his back to the room. When we appeared with Elmer, both men turned and ambled over. We'd put our arms through Elmer's just for fun, and waited to be introduced.

"Whoa, Elmer, what in Christ is going on?"

Their names were Vern and Tony. Vern was as small as Elmer. He jangled like a set of keys. I assumed he was held together by loose screws and rusty bolts. His face was tarnished as his medals, though his eyes glinted with light. Like he was peering out from a car wreck. Tony was younger, late sixtyish maybe, with a beer belly, a jowly chin and red-rimmed, rheumy eyes. Like he was peering out from, well, a pig. After he spoke, he kept staring at me, even when Elmer was introducing Linda to him. Don't know if he was shocked by the Goth getup, or thought I was going to pick his pockets. Linda always got mad at this type, the looks of longing and suspicion, as if our Goth business was evidence of ulterior motives, darker than the need for money. "They think they're so superior," Linda said. I used to argue this was okay, their condescension, I mean. We were like hookers, and people always condescend to those who profit from desire. Of course, the nature of the desire we were exploiting was, well, mysterious. Required a trick of the mind, not the body. We couldn't know what people really thought. And these guys were old enough to be our smelly grandfathers, anyway.

Once we'd settled on the couch, Vern and Tony brought us three Cokes before resuming their dart game. Elmer sat between us and started right in. War stories, of course. Linda leaned away, fixed her eyes on something across the room. Her job was to stay detached; mine was to show interest, though in a quiet way. Linda said that it was okay to talk, but that we should let the client do most of it. And it was better if their jive remained superficial. When the old guy began gushing out his stories, I knew Linda wouldn't like it. But I did. After all, this guy was pantin' hard, fogging up the one-eyed peephole of death's door.

"Never killed anybody," Elmer said (felt my interest drop, *death* erased from *sex and death*). "Least, not that I know. Never had to shoot a man face to face, anyway. Worse thing that happened: we were sweeping Caen, Normandy, 1945. Artillery softened it. Still on edge. Snipers. I was in the first group. Stepped into a bombed-out building, broken stone, glass, everywhere. Sudden noise. Caught something, corner of my eye. Swung round, believed some sniper had me dead to rights. Fired. Killed a little dog. Poor thing had survived the shelling. Fur grey with smoke. Red eyes. Tongue lolling out. Worst day of the war for me. Never felt so bad before or since. Took that wee thing, bundled it like a baby, buried it outside the town. Named it Mr. Pearson. In commemoration, you see. Imagine, naming something after it's dead."

Elmer asked us to raise our glasses, toast the dead dog. Death back on the agenda. He could hardly lift his. Nearly dumped his Coke on my corset (that's a phrase you won't hear often). He wilted. Mouth went slack, slobbery. Tongue lolling out. Put his hand, burn-shiny, on Linda's arm. She peeled it off, as if removing a vampire leech. Tony broke the tension by suggesting we play darts, that he'd snap a picture. We obliged and Elmer cheered up. We formed another tableau—the Goth Girls of Banff and two old soldiers set against 1970s wood-panelling, grouped by an old dart board, metal grid rusted and warped. I joked that our fingernails were long, sharp, detachable. We didn't need darts. Linda even showed talent for the game, releasing her darts in short order and scoring big, as if she'd been playing her whole life.

Goth Girls of Banff. Want a dark Victorian Doll for the day? Need to import a little Celtic twilight into your alpenglow? Need a quick raven girl to fly amidst your wolves and bears? We'll pose before a mountain stream. We'll perch on a mountaintop or ride a scree. We'll cast long shadows in the sunburnt mountain air. We'll even weep over your dead dog, throw darts with your fading buddies in a dank legion hall. Anything is possible, prices negotiable.

AFTER, LINDA SAID, "CAN'T GET THAT OLD WOLF OUT OF MY mind."

I said, "We can't stop clients from talking. It's their money."

"Creeps me out. I don't know what happens, it's sick nostalgia. Notice it's always older guys that hire us? Working stuff out."

"They're lonely is all."

"It's more than loneliness."

"Loneliness is *always* more. It's never simple. It's like this place. Loneliness is a whole mountain range."

"War stories. Everybody's got one. Wasn't bad once we started playing darts. That's the ticket, keep them distracted."

"You were good. You threw hard. Almost knocked the board off the wall."

"Felt good."

LINDA GOT THE GOTH GIRLS IDEA SIX YEARS AGO. We'd followed Mom out on a ski trip, her first since the divorce. Mom and Dad were always going on ski trips, though all we'd ever hear about was how funny Don Lapena was, of Don and Donna, their "priceless" friends in Calgary, he was the Canadian Vice-President of something or other, and whose chalet they stayed in in Banff. (Linda always said *After you eat, do they give you little bowls to rinse your hands*?) Linda didn't want to come, though it was the first time Mom was going alone. Still remember the argument:

"You can't stay with Dad, there's no room, and Christine's away. Not leaving you alone for two weeks."

"Don't want to go to Banff."

"It's gorgeous. Can't you be supportive, for once?"

"Want to be with my friends."

"What friends? Rachel? Anna Zymbrowski? I thought you weren't talking to them?"

"You don't know anything."

"Linda, if you want to bring a friend, bring two friends, I'd be happy to pay. It could be fun...."

"Not my idea of fun."

"If Dad was going, we were *all* going, would you go then?"

"Who cares," Linda said.

Linda was still upset about the divorce, even after a year. Well, not the divorce as such, though it sucked, but the fact that Mom and Dad had never really said anything, and suddenly their separation arrived, out of the blue, like a package from Purolator, both of them smiling like idiots when it came, trying to explain in low, reasonable voices. We knew they had big fights, like any couple, but "irreconcilable differences"—*come on*. Didn't help that Linda was going through a late high-school activist phase, where even the idea of skiing, of mountains shaved of trees for entertainment, not to mention that Banff was *A scar on the face of wilderness*, rankled her. She insisted that she wouldn't change her style for Banff. In fact, her style would be a wilderness symbol of mourning. It was going to be *Full Battle Goth Wear*, even at the chalet, no matter what.

Later, on the trip, while we were shopping for ski stuff in a little boutique on Banff Avenue, Linda refused to go in. She stood on the snowy sidewalk, smoking without a cigarette. (She wouldn't risk getting caught by Mom, but mimed the motion, in some vague gesture of rebellion.) She was wearing her priestess floor-length coat with buttons down the front, and high buckled stiletto boots. Her face was painted white, eyes and lips drawn in careful black, with a small upside-down cross like a teardrop on one cheek. Even with her boots planted firmly and with surliness cramping her upper lip, tourists kept stopping to look, like she was the store mascot. Bunch of skiers, all post-slope ruddy and exuberant, asked if they could take a picture with her, were chased off by her scowl. But a little girl, tiny version of Pippi Longstocking, ran right up to her, hugged her knees, until the girl's young dad apologized. He said Linda looked *awesome*, then also asked for a photo, his daughter with the *Dark Princess*. A black light went on over Linda's head then, she could exploit the people exploiting the wilderness, and the rest is Gothic history. I think our success has partly to do with the sound of it, *Goth Girls of Banff*, those double gs and fs. There's something Gothic, Germanic, in the name Banff, the two fs like vampire fangs. And even the Banff Springs Hotel, plunked down in the middle of the mountains, resembles Dracula's castle, or what I imagine it might look like.

Elmer Spragge had made an impression. That night, after our meeting with the old soldiers, Linda had a nightmare where she was tied down by a troop of withered men in boy scout uniforms, bound like Gulliver by dozens of tiny strings, and a three-headed dog, also dressed as a scout, was eating her arms, taking tiny, slow bites.

Startled out of bed, throwing her arms in front to be sure she still had them, she switched on the light in our rental flat and said, "That was too real. I can still *smell* the thing. We've gotta get real jobs." But the next week was the one that really ended it for Linda, forcing me to get a new partner, though nobody could ever replace my big sister: *Goth Girls of Banff. Not for the faint of heart. Put your hand where it shouldn't be, you'll lose it. Reminisce, or tear up when you talk, we'll lop your head off, hoist it on a dripping stick. Claim you want comfort, we'll cut out your wanking tongue. Kick you till you're dead. Goth Girls of Banff. That's enough. Don't make it more.*

ON LINDA'S SECOND LAST DAY, WE MET THIS GUY BY the Mount Rundle trailhead. He wanted to go hiking with us, then photograph us from the top of the mountain, the Banff Springs Hotel as backdrop. I was wearing a short Lilith dress, with chiffon webs and mesh sleeves, fishnet stockings and commando boots. Linda wore a Morticia skirt, a long-sleeve punk top with bell cuffs and a vest. Linda told the park warden at the Visitor Centre about our plans and gave her the guy's name and particulars, a precaution we always took when going off the beaten path with a client. But, no worries, Linda could be tough as coffin nails. Last year, she twisted one guy's arm up between his shoulders after he'd slipped his hand into her skirt, then got another three hundred bucks off him for not going to the RCMP. And we always carried pepper spray, in case of bears. But the bears were less a concern than the men.

The guy looked like Elvis Costello, *My Aim Is True*-era. He had a mop of black hair with some streaks of grey, and the dead-spiders trace of a goatee, and big black framed glasses. He wore army surplus shorts and a T-shirt that already had looping sweat stains under the arms, and his socks were blinding white, pulled right up to the bulbs of his knees. Though he had some strength in his face, his demeanour said something else, and I could see that Linda thought the same. Just as the hard black line we made when my sister and I glided through town seemed to repeat the phrase *Goth Girls of Banff*, his shy movement, and the way he was dressed, spoke one word: *Victim*. He may as well have had it tattooed on his forehead.

Some other hikers appeared at the trailhead: a short woman and a shorter man, followed by a gangly teenage boy, whose face was pinched red. As soon as they saw us, the man did a double take, and the woman said, her voice sounding a little folksy, a little Maritime, "My, this is wonderful. You look great, do you mind, can we get a picture with you two sweet girls?"

We spread apart, we knew the drill, left room for the couple between us. The boy took the digital camera from his father and said, his voice flinty, he was running roughshod over some previous emotion, "Isn't the Goth thing kind of dead?" Without missing a beat Linda said, "The undead never die." We both put on our best Goth deadpan. He took the photo. "Judy will think we went to *Transylvania*," the woman said, while the father, annoyed at his son's rudeness, snatched the camera from him, winked at us and chased his son down the trail. The mother sauntered after them, easy as rhubarb pie.

Our client introduced himself as Will. "About a two hour hike, there and back," he said in a deep voice like an actor's. It echoed big, it was wide and white-capped as the Bow River rapids, it didn't go with his geeky appearance.

Linda opened her eyes wide at me, crossed and rolled them, while Will stomped on the ground, dust hugging his calves. He waited, motioned for Linda to take the lead, fell in behind her. I followed. This formation was typical for us: most guys wanted to be between us, like the filling of a Goth sandwich.

Linda was excited by the hike, by the mountain air. That, and the fact she didn't relish the idea of actually talking to our client, pushed her forward. On the first couple of switchback turns, I could see, through her heavy makeup, the glow in her face. Her stride, too, was long, determined. Will couldn't keep up. On the fourth switchback, less than a third of the way, he stopped and offered me a drink from the silver bottle he unclipped from his pack. I jabbed a thumb towards my own pack. He grinned when he saw it was shaped like a coffin. "Your partner's sure anxious to get gone," he said. I almost said *sister*, but didn't. Something furry crept up my back, prickled along my neck, and I caught a whiff that reminded me of Elmer Spragge. I could always feel the questions coming. "How'd you get started doin' this? Why do people, you know, hire you?"

I wanted to say he could answer his own question. Didn't he have friends, family of his own? Normal hobbies to occupy his time? Why did *he* hire us? He was a nerdy snake chewing his own tail. But I always fell back on Linda's advice, that the client liked it best when their questions went unanswered. "Fell into it by accident," I said. "Don't know why, it's a mystery to us, too." Took a hit from my water bottle, used a towel to wipe the bruise from the rim. Wished Linda hadn't rushed ahead, though I suspected she was watching. When Will moved closer, I stepped off the trail, wedged myself between two trees so he'd have no room to sidle. Linda taught me the manoeuvre. But he only took his glasses off, twisted the heels of his hands into his brow as if tightening screws.

"You ladies remind me…." he began, but his voice broke. He *was* about to share something. I cut in, "We need to get going. We have another gig today." I felt mean. But this is what they wanted, Linda said. They needed us to be cool and distant. I stepped out from the trees, posed a little, stood pigeon-toed, stretched my arms, let my wide-screen sleeves hang. He watched, and perhaps understood—it was about the pose, the image. That was all that was on offer, for now.

When we rounded the turn, I saw that Linda was giving better than me. She was perched on a rock, one leg pushed forward, the other thrust behind, one lacy arm along her side, the other up in an arc, her hand plucking sweat from her forehead then sprinkling the seeds. Set against the greenness, she was a primping bird, and stood that way a long minute, letting Will watch. She blasted off again. The idea was to get properly spaced, twelve feet between us, so that Will would get his money's worth but be too winded to talk. He kept slowing so that I had to adjust my pace.

Wasn't long before we were a few switchbacks from the top of the trail. The aching blue sky had grown and I could see weather in the treetops. Saw, too, that my lace gloves were worn and my fishnets had rents in them. We'd use the day's Goth earnings to repair our battle gear.

Will halted above me on the trail. I stopped too and peered into the woods. Didn't want to catch up to him, pretended something caught my eye. He came back down, said, "You okay?"

"Thought I saw an animal," I lied. "Wolf or something.

Sunlight on fur." Where was Linda? Why didn't she wait when she saw we'd stopped?

Will didn't follow my gaze down into the woods, said, looking straight up, as if expecting Wile E. Coyote to drop an anvil on him, "Saw a wolf once, me and my wife, in Jasper. In a clearing by the trail. Yellow eyes. When she took out her phone to get a shot, it was gone. Like into a hole in the ground."

He had a look of polished blankness on his face, as if his features had disappeared. Like into a hole in the ground. Thought of asking him why he was alone, where was his wife, but said, as if I hadn't noted his vacancy, "Yeah, wolves are quick. There one second, etc. Like my sister." I flinched a little at having said *sister*, felt as if this tiny deception—it wasn't deception really, he didn't need to know we were sisters—added to whatever hurt he was feeling. I took some steps up the trail, turned around to see he'd crouched down. I said, "Whatever it is, it'll pass. We gotta keep up, though." I went back, offered my hand.

Pulled him standing. His cheeks were wet, I wouldn't go there. Why didn't I ask what the matter was? He was a stranger, yes. A client. But in an hour, we'd never have to see him again. Linda would murder me if we got trapped listening, she didn't need any more nightmares, any more dead dogs. I strode ahead, let him fade. We were nearly done, anyway.

THE TREES WERE SMALL AND STUNTED NOW, BRISTLING LIKE bonsai. Elmer Spragge's hands. The trail ended at a big limestone wall, below the mountain's peak. We'd gone as far as we could, though I knew it wasn't far enough for Will. Linda, backed up against the pale scoured stone, looked fantastic, the way her sleeves dripped as she leaned back and chugged from her black water bottle, the way her black hair, caught in a breeze, feathered against the rock. No wonder people wanted to be near us. There was pleasure in the looking. I sat on a lightning-struck boulder near her, its two halves in a perfect yin-yang, looked down to see that the tops of my fishnets were caked in dust, a filigree of gunmetal like medieval chainmail. We heard this booming sigh, and Will appeared from the last trail bend. Bent over almost double, he was leading with a glistening bald spot. The hike was too much for him. I stood. Linda grabbed my wrist, held me back, whispered, "Don't."

"Bitch," I almost said, though there'd be love in the syllable.

Will managed to stand, sank again. He muttered, more air than words, "Tough hike. I wasn't expecting, you girls none the worse for wear...."

Linda said quickly, "We're vets. Catch your breath, but we need to be back in half an hour."

Will kept breathing through his mouth, his face a squished, palpitating mass, his arms wrapped around his knees, eyes closed. When he opened them, they bulged with water, effect magnified through his glasses. Impossible to ignore. But Linda was trying. She turned and put her hands against the stone wall, began to do upright push-ups, limbering herself for our descent, and it meant *Don't indulge him, I'll leave you with him if you ask him what the matter is.* Caught in his watery gaze, I couldn't ignore him. I *was* a Goth Girl of Banff but I wasn't my sister, bit my lip till it hurt, till I tasted blood. Then said, softly, "You all right? What's wrong, is it, is the hike too much?"

Was relieved when he said, "Nothing. I'm good. No worries."

He stood and took his glasses off and rubbed his eyes, washed the dusty hair on his forearm. Looked at me. He was resisting something and I could see he expected that I would ask. It was a kind of game, he was being manly, stoic, and he made a stoic pose, like an athlete fighting off pain. When I thought he'd succeeded, and just as Linda walked towards us, ready to lead, he said, new tears glinting in his eyes, "My wife was killed in these mountains. First time I've been back, since."

I looked at Linda. Her face was hard as the rock behind us. But something quivered in her eye, maybe the reflection of a bird—a whisky-jack had begun to follow us up the trail, looking for handouts—or a bubble of glacial water that would eventually erode the stone of who she was, who she was trying to be. I saw our dad standing there, trying to explain. Still, Linda didn't speak, so I said, "That's terrible." And, thinking on my feet, Linda had taught me well, "Why don't you tell me about it on the way down?"

He snapped to attention, said to Linda, "Could you take a picture of Jessie and me, against the rock?" Found his cellphone, held it out to her. She was glad for this distraction. Will and I backed up against the mountain, faced the squinting sun. He put his arm around my waist, let his hand rest close to my butt. I didn't mind, though I could feel his fingers, like he needed to scratch an itch. This was the crux of it; this is what some men did; this is how they dealt with anguish, sad memory turning into lust, grief into desire, a prickling hollow shock that started in the chest but gathered in the groin. This is what kept some folks going in the midst of loss. I wondered, suddenly, where my sadness was hiding, what I was doing to ignore it.

Linda made short work of the photo, but as soon as the image appeared in the little oblong, Will burst into tears. His arm tightened around my waist. Obliged by proximity, I turned and gave him a quick hug, then broke it off, repeating, "It's okay, tell me what happened." Linda was already descending.

As he began, I saw that Linda slowed her pace, not wanting to let me take the full brunt of his story. But I was perfectly capable of handling him alone.

"She died near here, in Yoho National Park. We were staying in a cabin, end of the valley. We'd finished a hike. I was tired, but she, my wife, was quite the athlete, wanted to hike again. Went alone. It was the spring of, I don't know. Three years ago. She was attacked. By wolves. One of only three cases in North America. Been a hard winter. The Park people shot the wolves, five of them. All I remember were the ravens. Ravens in the trees. Hate those scavengers. We had a ceramic raven that her sister, an artist, made us as a wedding gift. I smashed it, threw it away."

As he told the story, his voice was unsteady, about to mudslide. I was aware of how Linda and I resembled ravens, the material beneath our arms catching the breeze, our tail feathers, our oily black hair. Began to wonder if this was why he hired us, maybe he was working things out, trying to forgive; we were ravens, figures of death he needed to rub up against. Or he meant us harm—hike the scavenging bitches onto the mountain then slit their throats. Serial killers always looked like him, too, meek and geeky, disguise for the seething rage.

"My God, that's awful, I'm so sorry," I said, trying so hard for sincerity that I sounded fake, though I was *totally* sincere.

He collected himself, pushed his shoulders forward then back. Smiled sheepishly. It was a half-smile, it was an apology for his show of emotion. It was then I felt really bad, seeing him work his way past grief. I was feeling bad for his feeling bad about feeling bad. Linda wasn't feeling bad. She had turned, was thumping down the trail. It was a directive—this was business, the way the ravens hovering around his dead wife was business, nothing more or less.

Once some time had passed, Linda let us catch up. But time hadn't softened things. His story felt heavier now. It was as if my awkward response, and my sister's silence, had added to the tragedy, as if the air had grown thicker because we hadn't responded with the appropriate pity and terror. Our professional attitude was an insult to the depth of his emotion. In fact, it was an insult to the whole reality of grief, as if all the sorrow that had ever been felt in these dark cathedral woods, in this part of the world, was mocked by these costumes, our Goth pose. Wanted to say to my sister, *Shouldn't the Gothic be a place where grief can live*? I hated our Gothness. We were a contradiction, a fraud.

I was astonished to see that these thoughts had found a place in my sister's expression. Or perhaps she'd seen the death-valley look on my face, was mirroring me. But there was real sorrow in the curve of her black mouth that I'd only seen once recently, when she was explaining how her six-month boyfriend Max had broken up with her with a text message: *your a great girl but neither of us can help it its not meant to be*. Whatever the reason, I knew that my sister couldn't have found it easy to lower her guard and say, "I'm sorry. That's terrible what happened. Our condolences. If there is anything we can do, just ask."

This was all the man needed. It allowed him to move on, at least in the short term of our hike. He nodded in a grateful way, put his glasses on again, and hiked on ahead of us, leading us both for the first time. I felt privileged. Linda wouldn't make eye contact with me, but there was a new lightness in her step. Maybe she had realized that it was possible to fit compassion into our Goth roles, that everything didn't have to conform to hard, dark fantasy.

AN HOUR LATER, WE WERE SITTING IN A LITTLE CAFÉ, Sourdough Stop, off of Banff's main street. We'd just deposited Will's cheque but weren't talking about him. I was admiring Linda's espresso, the abrupt little cup, and she was examining her fingernails, yellow veins in the chipped blackness, when something chirped. Chirped again. Maybe Linda had a tiny bird caught up in the webs of her dress, or a vampire bat. Her eyes widening, she reached into the pocket of her vest, pulled out Will's cellphone. "Oh fuck," she said, then shoved it at me, saying, "It's probably him, wants his phone back. Tell him you'll leave it at the Visitor Centre. Bet he forgot it on purpose." I scowled at my sister, though wasn't surprised she'd tamed her compassion so quickly.

I snapped it open, put my face into the V. After a silence, a female voice said, "Is Will there? Who is this?"

"I'm a friend. Not a friend, exactly. Will isn't here. He forgot his phone. I'm just answering it."

"Yeah, I can hear that. So who are you?"

"Ummm, I'm not really. You see, Will hired us. That doesn't sound right. We're the *Goth Girls of Banff*. We run a business. We went for a hike with him, that's all, and he forgot his phone."

"Goth Girls of Banff? Really? You're kidding. Ha, I've heard of you. You know, I was something of a Goth in high school, though more punk. Joy Division, Siouxsie and the Banshees, you know. My *husband* hired you?"

I covered the phone with my hand, said to Linda, "It's his wife," started to giggle, said into the phone, "Yes, he hired us. You're his wife? Your husband implied that you were no longer, ah, in the picture."

I realized this was the wrong thing to say, but she said, "Sometimes I wish. Told you I was dead, did he? What was it this time? Car accident? Struck by lightning? Mauled by a bear? It's always something gruesome."

I lowered the phone, gasped at Linda, who said, "What? What?" I spoke into the phone again, said, deadpan, "You were eaten by wolves."

"Uh-huh. My name's Deb. My husband is a bit of a character. Bit of a dick, some would say. He's an actor. When he's preparing for a role, he likes to go off and improvise, test things out. He likes to play off real people. Sorry. I'm not dead."

"Don't be sorry."

I felt ridiculous. Excited, too. We talked for a while longer. She had lots of questions and kept apologizing for them, said she hadn't talked to anyone, except her parents, in weeks. She and Will lived in Canmore, just outside of Banff. She worked part-time at the Safeway there. Her father had worked for several years at a motor lodge in Rogers Pass, and her mother worked in Rescue Operations for the Park Warden Service. Both were retired. She and Will lived with them. She told me she was looking for something to supplement her income. Will, she complained, brought in next to nothing as an actor, though he'd recently played a bit part in a CBC movie about the 1982 Canadian Everest Expedition that was filmed in the Rockies. He'd met William Shatner. I arranged to drop off the phone the following afternoon, and she suggested we have a coffee, there was a great place in Canmore. To think I'd be having coffee with a dead woman.

Once the call ended, I explained everything to Linda. I talked loosely and fast. I thought it was funny we'd been played. After all, we were playing him, weren't we? But Linda swallowed her espresso in one gulp, slammed the cup down on the pine table, left a dent in the wood and black scar from her lipstick all around the cup's rim. She snatched at her hair and closed her eyes, and when she opened them again, black tears streamed down her face. She said, almost spitting, causing the other patrons to fall silent, "I didn't even want to *listen* to his shit. We don't pretend to be something we're not."

I thought of saying *Sure we do*, but thought better of it, under the circumstances—I was surprised and scared at her anger, though I knew she'd given something up in her empathy with the client, that even in her brief moment of compassion she'd paid too high a price. It was then I knew for sure that her days as a *Goth Girl of Banff* were done. There was a chink in her Goth armour, and this had been revealed, not in response to reality, but to an actor's story. I think this was what bothered her. At least, this was part of it. Other parts I didn't understand. Wolves? Turns out Linda was the one who'd been devoured.

OUR LAST CLIENTS THAT FINAL REQUIEM DAY WERE TWO young men, serious vampire enthusiasts. They showed up for our Banff Springs brunch more elaborately dressed than we were, wearing Lord Byron shirts with weeping sleeves, tight elastic pants and strappado boots that reached to their knees, and their thin faces painted cadaverously, hair teased up into smoking volcanoes. During the meal, and as they took pictures of us all together on the hotel patio, Linda didn't say a word, but the two guys didn't seem to mind, understood we were playing our Goth roles. Linda ate her sunny-side-up eggs as if they were accusing eyes, and cut her sausage into mean little bits, her steak knife scraping the plate. The guys didn't notice, didn't care, they were better Goths than us. After a few photos, the couple disappeared into the brick corridors of the hotel, and, before I'd had a chance to talk to her, Linda also vanished. I imagined she'd flapped up and away and was tucked in under one of the towers of the hotel, moulting in darkness high above the Bow Valley. Later, she wouldn't talk about her Goth career. It was as if those days were just a bad dream, or a grief long forgotten, buried by time and circumstance.

I love my sister. I miss her, our Goth time together.

AFTER OUR MEETING WITH THE VAMPIRE COUPLE, I WENT TO return the cellphone to Will's wife Debbie, who became my new partner. She had great ideas, immediately worked to lift our Goth profile. Before long, we had a line of *Goth Girls of Banff* T-shirts, gloves, hats and sun visors, coffee mugs, and computer mouse pads. (My favourite is a graphic of both of us looking our Goth best, towering over a cowering grizzly bear.) We got most of the local stores to carry our merchandise, and we always make an appearance at the Banff Winter Carnival, sometimes snuggling up against the Banff Santa Claus. Now, there are twelve of us, so Debbie and I do the administrivia, while our employees, our Goth Team, go out into the field. And though we aren't trained as counsellors, one of our team, Seema Ray, has a degree in psychology, so led us through some informal workshops. We encourage our clients to talk, to share, to bond with us—it's amazing what people will share with a woman in funereal garb, our extreme dress encouraging the erasing of boundaries—although we still maintain some professional distance and make referrals if necessary. Oh, and my sister Linda? She went on to do a history degree at York University in Toronto, has become an authority on the role of women during the Great War. And though she doesn't like to talk about our Goth Girl days, sometimes, on Halloween, she'll put on her old Goth stuff and parade in front of her kids, who screech with embarrassment.

NATURAL SELECTION

BIG MISTAKE TO DRAG MY DRUNK BROTHER TO THE mountains. But this ain't really true, as my brother never actually made it to the mountains. What I wouldn't give now to heft and heave the mountains to him. Fairer to say, he just couldn't make it and I can't face the heavy lifting. Bruised, bandaged, and hooked up, a skinny, pale, poisoned thing, he's in a hospital in Calgary. Unless my sis Emma and brother-in-law Dan have lent him the bum's rush, put him on a plane, packed him back east. Or he's on another bender in some cowboy bar, hospital bracelet sliding from his wrist, ringing the neck of a bowling-pin-sized bottle of rye. Or my sister has throttled him to death, in retaliation for him traumatizin' her cat, after what the cat did to him. But given the nature of things, what does it matter? I'm watching a pack of wolves steal a moose calf from its mom, drag it onto the blinding shore, and devour it. They throw their arrow heads back. Blood fans from their snouts. Sun grins behind the red screen.

"EMMA, DON'T THINK I FORGET," RONNY SAID OVER DINNER that first night. He kept his eyes on his salmon, poking the white and pink meat with his thumb.

"Ronny, we talked about this," I said, my teeth together.

Emma's husband let his fork screech across his plate and stood up. When Dan stood up, you noticed: tall and redwood-wide with a wide and elongated skull and long jaw. My first idea of him, some twenty years before, was that he looked like Frankenstein, though, okay, in one of the monster's better moments.

Dan's napkin flew from his lap and draped the butter. "Forget what?" he said, stepping out, face gone red like the cherries Emma had on deck for dessert. The silver candelabrum, branches for seventeen candles, blocked his view, and Dan wanted to look Ronny, no-bullshit, straight in the eyes.

"You were in no condition. When you're better, the money will be there."

I thought it real kind that Dan didn't say, spitting out the words in liquid force, *When you're sober*. Red in the face, yes, but Dan was holdin' back.

Ronny lifted a chunk of salmon, squeezed it between his dry pursed lips. He had that bleak, *I'm used to this* look. EmmaDan's Siamese cat Mindy—this is what we called them, *EmmaDan*, since they hightailed it out west, like they were one person, like Emma had no say in the matter—chose that moment to leap into Ronny's lap.

"Keep her there," Emma said. "Don't pat her. She bites." Ronny leaned forward, gently pinned the animal to the table. She twisted a little, calmly licked the edge of his plate.

Emma came over and Ronny sat back. She scooped Mindy up, dropped her with a soft thud to the hardwood. The cat paused, stared back at Ronny. She looked prehistoric, boney, and blue-tinged, and had a big triangular head with huge veined ears. Emma told us, when the weird creature had greeted us at the door, that she was a "Wedgehead," a modern Siamese that, sadly, had a short life span. Ronny pulled his chair close to the table. The scraping sound (I imagined EmmaDan having their hardwood done a month ago, all the dough they forked out, I nearly guffawed) made Dan give a loud exhale. Holding back again, he exchanged a look with Emma.

"It was for the best," said Emma. "But we're glad you're here. We're happy you're *both* here." With both hands she reached across the table, but Ronny didn't respond. She squeezed my hand and smiled, but had a crease in her forehead that looked like a fossil in stone, like the ones on display at the Calgary airport. I tried to remember if it had always been there. Couldn't.

Ronny nodded and went back to his food. His poached salmon was gone, but he hadn't touched the pile of wild rice, or the three sad sticks of asparagus. Ronny, since we were kids, had always eaten his meals slowly, one food group at a time, as if he couldn't trust the whole idea of food and had to eat carefully, fearfully.

"This is good," he said. His tiny olive branch. Probably the most they were going to get out of him.

"No worries, we understand," Emma said.

Dan didn't look like *he* understood. He was mirroring Ronny in his focus on his plate. The candelabrum was suddenly like a great cage between them—a cage full of air, maybe lost rack of antlers, and a breeze from somewhere was fanning its flames.

WHILE WE UNPACKED IN THE GUEST ROOM, I WENT A BIT Rottweiler, snapped at Ronny. He was yanking sweaters and oily T-shirts from a green duffle bag like he was ripping apart a carcass.

"Christ Ronny, we're guests, if that means anything. Thought you were all right with things."

"Never said that."

"You did. You said *I'm all right with things*. Asked you before I bought the tickets. Asked you a week ago. Asked you at the airport."

"Don't remember."

Wanted to say, *That's what booze does to your brain*. Said, "Why would I even bring you out here if I thought...."

"Let's get out of here, go downtown."

"You wanna drink? Didn't you promise Marcia? EmmaDan don't mind if you have a beer. But we don't want what happened at Easter...."

"They weren't there."

"They know what happened."

"Bitch Magda. Or did you tell them?"

"You threatened her, Ronny. How could I not say anything?"

"That's why they were so glad to see me."

"*Are* glad to see you, asshole. Anyway, we got some exploring to do. Got two days to get you in shape. Hey, brother, let's chill, enjoy ourselves. Look at this."

I pulled back the white lace curtains, expecting to see mountains on the horizon. They were gone. The view had changed since my last visit: second floors and third floors, tall French windows, wide rooftop decks, and stupid castle turrets added to the older bungalows and ranch houses in the neighbourhood. But Ronny didn't care to look, just kept dragging stuff from his bag, everything twisted, knotted together. There was a ripe smell. After five minutes the stink was still strong.

"Ronny, didn't you wash your stuff?"

"Forgot."

"You still going to AA? When was the last time you went?"

"Guy got stabbed in our laundry room last year."

"Thought Marcia was keeping you on track?"

"She ain't in charge of me."

I sighed and said, "Put them back. Maybe we can contain the gorgeous smell."

Ronny began to replace his clothes, moving so crippled I figured he was hurt, cut by my comment. Then I saw him sniff and flinch, as if he really didn't know. I thought of saying sorry, but just nodded at him, uselessly.

EMMADAN WERE IN THE DEN WATCHING A RERUN OF *TAXI*. Both smiled as I came in. Dan's shoulders relaxed when he saw Ronny wasn't with me. I told them that Ronny's things were a bit, ah, *funky*. Could we, sorry, do a laundry? In the basement, Emma's forehead fossil vanished. She was happy to slip away from her husband, what with all his moods, though she said, in this case, she didn't blame him. He had no patience, she said, for her family, though, according to her, Dan liked *me* well enough. On this trip, Ronny was the sour part of a package deal.

"You should get some medal for bringing him out here," she said. "Not sure, though, I understand why."

"His prostate treatments went well, but you know. Everybody should see the mountains before they die."

There was an old battered drum kit in the corner of the room—cymbals floating and leaking pink pillows stuffed into the bass drum—in the one place in their basement that hadn't been renovated, wires and bare pipes that looked like percussion instruments, part of the kit.

"I take it those are Kevin's? Where is he, I thought we'd see him?"

Emma put down Ronny's bag. "We bought him a brand new set. Beautiful. Expensive. Of course he hated it. Wanted something, he said, with history. He's away. At a friend's in the Okanagan. Or so he tells us. I don't ask too many questions. He's applying to college in the fall. He's a good drummer. Dan won't let him practice when we're home though. Says he's wasting his time. Course, that goes over *real* well."

Emma picked up Ronny's bag, unzipped it, pulled out a pair of pants, dropped the bag again. "Good Lord, did he poop himself? This smells like a dead dog."

"Dead dog soaked in vinegar."

"Dead dog soaked in vinegar and set on fire."

"Dead dog soaked in vinegar and set on fire and wearing Ronny's flaming underwear."

"You've gone too far," she said and we both laughed. Then she screamed, scared piss out of me, started to shake, whipped the pants against the wall, tossed them into the front-loading washer, dumped the rest of Ronny's clothes out, scooped them into the hole, made fists with her hands and face, steadied herself on the machine. She was tilting and rattling. She was on spin cycle. She grabbed a tub of liquid detergent, unscrewed the lid and tipped it over an open slot, but spilled blue liquid all over the floor. "Pray for me," she said. "Okay. Okay. It'll be all right."

"Emma, what the hell is it?"

She looked at me like I was dumb, like Dan looked at Ronny. "Tell Ronny to get undressed. Dan'll give him pajamas. Where are his shoes? Dan's gonna kill him. You better change. Bathrobe on our bedroom door. Take your clothes off."

"Emma…."

"*Bedbugs*. Love of Christ, that's all we need."

WE SAT IN THE LIVING ROOM, RONNY WEARING DAN'S pajamas, they were too big and made him look like a little shit, like that evil kid in *The Omen*. He was sitting real straight, head up, feet flat on the floor, arms on the armrests, as if how straight he sat might fix things. I sat next to Emma on the couch, my knees together and arms crossed to keep my bathrobe from spilling open. There'd already been enough shocks for one day.

Dan sat in the chair across from Ronny. He had on a dress shirt, a white linen one buttoned high at the throat, though at dinner he'd been casual, with a V-neck sweater over a white T-shirt. I figured his dressing up was a criticism of his wife's brothers. Emma had changed too, was wearing black silk Chinese-type sweatpants and a top with a pattern of herons. She looked like a flower. Her clothes were scolding us too.

I was thinking about the bedbugs. Thinking about how I'd seen them on the airplane, little critters jumping and partying and toasting with tiny red martinis on Ronny's shoulders as he slept, but that it was too late to do anything about it. By the time we'd gone through the rigamarole of getting our luggage and renting the car, I'd forgot about them. Or maybe I didn't. Maybe I was bad as Ronny.

Dan tried to move things along, though he coughed before he spoke, like he'd swallowed some bedbugs. "What are your plans in the mountains? Are you hiking? I assume you want something easy."

He was right about that. I was just glad he didn't bring up the bedbugs, how shitty it was that I came with more than one unwelcome guest.

"We'll hike the Bow. I'm not in good shape. And we need to, what do they say, *acclimatize*. We're at a higher elevation here than in Toronto."

"Maybe the bedbugs'll die then," Ronny announced. He didn't change from his stiff pose, legs pulled tight against his chair.

Emma looked at Dan. Dan stared at Ronny, burned a hole in him. Ronny looked at Mindy, who was licking her bum near Ronny's chair. I looked at Dan. It looked as though he was watching Ronny do what Mindy was doing. Silence and big awkwardness, big as EmmaDan's washing machine, like it was sitting smack in the middle of the rug. Ronny didn't help things when he said, looking back at Dan now, "You have this weird cat, right? I mean, don't she bring in mice and stuff? Ticks, fleas? Or don't you care, in *her* case?"

"Cats are clean," Dan said. "*Animals* are very clean."

Emma was burnin' a hole in Ronny. Though her face looked like it was gonna burst into flame. Dan saw this, closed his eyes, stood. I thought he was gonna punch Ronny. I wondered if Ronny would explode into dust. No, he'd burst into a fountain of *al-kee-hall*. Ronny glared up at him, a challenge, but Dan said to Ronny, surprising everyone, maybe even himself, "You want a beer? Air's dry here, you're probably dehydrated."

I thought at first he was talking down to Ronny, but his tone was easy. Maybe he'd felt Ronny's embarrassment. He knew Ronny better than I thought he did, how the weather of Ronny's life was a series of windy gusts, mistakes and embarrassment followed by gusts of *Fuck you*, followed by embarrassment again, confirmation of his worthlessness, then some indifference, exhaustion, followed by *Fuck you* again. Maybe he was trying to push Ronny into his "indifferent" phase, hoping this would settle things. Or Dan, seeing that Ronny had switched into embarrassment, had offered him a beer knowing he'd refuse. Dan, too, was one-upping my sister, his wife. She let herself get furious at Ronny and swung between total disgust and a kind of sticky understanding. No middle ground for Emma. She was a simple girl, though she acted like she wasn't. She'd condemn then forgive, condemn then forgive. But always way outside of Ronny, in a whole other world.

"Sure," Ronny said.

"Believe I'll have one myself," said Dan.

While Dan and Ronny started discussing beer on the market, all the new craft brands, I joined my sis in the basement as she moved our laundry into the dryer. After, we sat on the flowery couch near the laundry room, under a buzzing fluorescent light and big colourful poster of the Kananaskis Ski Resort. My sister, still angry, forced her anger into the tighter shape of accusation.

"Really, Mark," she started, and I knew I was in for it, I was goin' straight into the washing machine. "Why'd you bring him here? You mad, too, about what happened with Dad's money?"

Knew this would come up. But I wasn't mad, never had been. "You guys deserved it," I said. "You lent them a lot of money back in the day."

"*Lent*? You got it wrong. Dad never paid us back. Didn't intend on paying us back. Dan practically bought their condo for them. So when Dad died...."

I cut her off, didn't need to hear it all again, "Emma, I know. Good thing Magda was the executor. I'm fine. Ronny'll be lucky to get a cent."

Emma put her hand on my arm then pushed it through her hair. Her brown hair was tied back, curly and dark but grey along the hairline. I fell back into the couch. I needed to show her I was perfectly content. I was, I really was, but the fact that EmmaDan might think otherwise made me tense up. Emma said, "Part of me thought you were bringing Ronny here to rub our faces in it. You've been a great help to him. You should get Ronny's share. I wish we could have been closer to home...."

"He's never been out of Toronto. I thought if he got away. Thought if he saw, you know, a real lake. A mountain. Might help him somehow. Settle him. You know. Nature. His girlfriend agrees with me."

"Girlfriend? You're kidding, right? Ronny has a *girlfriend*?"

"Marcia. Sorry, I thought you knew. Guess Magda only tells you the shit. He met her a few months ago, at the Scott Mission, when he went through that bad patch. She volunteers there. She's great. She's Native. Cree, I think. I haven't met her, only talked to her on the phone, but Ronny says, since he met her, he's really cut back on his drinking."

"Scott Mission? Doesn't he get social assistance?"

"Not enough. I help him out, too, now and then. No big deal."

Emma got up, went over and crouched in front of the dryer to watch the tumbling clothes. "I'm so embarrassed. I really don't know much about his life."

"Well, this is your chance," I said. Though I knew that my brother's life was, even to me, mysterious, only the broad strokes of it on display.

That night, Ronny and I didn't talk, didn't discuss the events of the day, even when we climbed into the same bed. I hid my irritation at how long he'd spent in the bathroom, though we were guests and I'd seen Emma hovering in the hall in her nightgown, listening at the bathroom door. But I was glad at how fresh my brother smelled, and that he still wore Dan's pajamas, so I didn't need to worry about brushing against his bare flesh in the night.

I WOKE TO SHOUTING. FUMBLED FOR, AND SWITCHED ON, THE bedside lamp, found that Ronny's side of the bed was empty. Digital clock glowed 3:20. Pulled on Dan's bathrobe, sat on the edge of the bed. Listened. Felt a little thrill, a sweet breathlessness. Went along the hall and down the carpeted stairs, all the while the angry words getting angrier, Dan's voice right up there, scratchin' the crown moulding.

I could hear Dan, but could see only Ronny. He was *on* the dining room table, sprawled across it face down, one leg sticking over the edge, the other folded on top. His pajama top was hiked up, he was bare-backed, jagged line of his spine visible. On the other end of the table were empty beer bottles, set up in a V like bowling pins, the point of the V a bottle of rye. Ronny's head was the bowling ball. He was out cold. I knew cause I heard a croak, Ronny's snore—he sounded exactly like a sandhill crane. (There were always sandhill cranes on this swamp near the cabin we stayed in as kids, when we were a great gang, Magda, Emma, Ronny, and me.) I watched a river forming on the table near his waist, spilling onto the hardwood. Dan didn't react, just went into the kitchen and came back with a wad of paper towels, shoved them under Ronny and on the floor beneath his stinking waterfall. The silver candelabrum was also on the floor, all the candles spilled out like trees from a mini clear-cut, and scattered among them were beer caps like tiny buzz saw blades.

I inhaled the beer and piss smell. Felt comforted by it, like Ronny was telling me a secret, whispering in my ear. Not sure what he was saying.

"More wilderness than you'll ever need," Dan said to me, spent now. He shook his head. "It's my fault."

I was surprised by that, gotta admit. Then, "He has a disease." But it was Emma speaking now, red tip of her cigarette jumping in the dark living room. "It's called *being an asshole*. You need to leave in the morning, get him out of here." I could barely see her, the room blurry with smoke, just the red cigarette glow, flaring and fading, flaring and fading, like an animal eye. I didn't know Emma smoked.

LATE MORNING, AND I WENT DOWN TO GET RONNY FROM the basement where we'd carried him, deposited him on the couch. Found him sitting at Kevin's drum kit, bare-chested, arms and chest and shoulders hairless and boney as the cat. He was faking playing the drums, eyes closed, drumsticks in his hands, but making the drumbeats and percussive sounds with his mouth, his version of Led Zeppelin's "Black Dog." Felt the urge to join him, to fall into sync with an air guitar, to windmill and howl and drop to my knees, to return to my teenage years in goofy solidarity. I didn't.

He'd collected and folded his laundry. It was laid out in neat piles on the drums. When he heard me, he stopped and opened his eyes and put his hands down, the drumsticks crossed in his lap.

I said, "What happened to your hand?"

There was a thick square wad of gauze on Ronny's right hand, wrapped round with white tape. I wondered if, in the night, he'd done himself more harm.

"Cat bit me last night. Can't say I blame her. Tried to get her to be my bowling ball."

"We're leaving. Can't stay here now. We'll get a room in the city. Don't have a place to stay in Banff till Friday."

"Sorry I screwed up."

"We're here for the mountains. But we gotta buy a gift, apologize to EmmaDan. Don't want Emma to see you today."

"She already has. Checked on me this mornin'. Patched up my hand."

"Least she could do," I said, making up my mind, then and there, that I blamed EmmaDan for what happened. They wouldn't hide their big supply of alcohol because, what Emma said anyway, this would have made it obvious they didn't trust Ronny. But their disgust leaked out in other ways, and was the thing that pushed him to fuck up. Maybe we'd all pushed him, me more than anyone. Maybe I had dragged Ronny west to "rub their faces in it" and Ronny knew this, was just doing what everyone expected him to do. Then Dan offered him that first beer. But I shoulda got more money when Dad kicked off. Since we were kids, I always got lumped in with Ronny, stuck in the same recycling bin, though I've never been without a job. Okay, jobs on the losin' end, but I always make my rent, never begged our parents, or Magda or EmmaDan, for anything.

I wondered if I should phone Marcia, tell her what happened, that Ronny had jumped, with both feet, off the wagon. But I decided not to—why give her stress, after all she'd done for him?

WE WENT TO THIS NEW MALL NEAR FISH CREEK PARK. Emma told me that she and Dan had protested its construction, cause it would disturb animal migration routes. I tried to think of something to buy for EmmaDan, but besides a new dining room table, couldn't think of anything. I kept Ronny close, and he kept suggesting food things. He brought over a huge hatbox full of shortbread, then a tower of Swiss chocolates. I explained that EmmaDan were health nuts. Next, he was carrying a wooden box of smoked salmon, a Haida design on it. I said this wasn't a bad idea. He suggested, too, floorin' me, that we buy a cedar plank, so they could use it later to barbecue salmon. I asked him how the hell he knew about using a cedar plank—I mean, the guy lived in a low-rent apartment near Regent Park in Toronto. His face went sort of blank, and at the same time I remembered Marcia, his Indigenous girlfriend. She'd probably introduced the idea.

Me and Ronny checked into a Motel 6. I picked one in the boonies, and on the way pretended I was lost. I wanted to make sure there were no bars or beer stores around. It was cool, too, cause we could see the mountains from the motel window. Ronny told me he was feeling sick. "What did you expect?" I said. He disappeared into the bathroom. Shower went on. Stayed on for a long time. I knocked on the door. When he finally came out, chased by curtains of steam, he was fully dressed again, looking exactly as he had before. "There are bathrobes," I said, looking forward to using one myself. He told me he wanted to sleep. While I flipped through the *Canadian Rockies Trail Guide*, Ronny stretched out on top of the squeaky bed covers in his ripped black jeans and Adidas sweatshirt, then curled into a tight ball. Once he was asleep, a sandhill crane nesting in the room, I yanked the quilt from the other side of the bed and folded it over him.

WANTED TO DROP OFF THE GIFT TO EMMADAN BEFORE WE LEFT for Banff the next day. Told Ronny he could sleep more, but he wanted to come. Wanted to apologize. He was in his embarrassment phase. I worried that, before we got there, he'd enter his fuck you phase. I wondered if I was still mad at EmmaDan too. Wanted to be, but wasn't sure why. It had something to do with their big candelabrum, with their skiing poster in the basement, with their SUV-sized washing machine. With their expensive prehistoric cat. With the drum kit, too. I had the feeling that EmmaDan might renovate right over it, that the drums and cymbals would disappear with the insulation and pipes in the wall.

On the way to their place, Ronny was looking bad, shiny and ragged, like a cloth soaked in turpentine. His breathing was loud. I told him we should go to a walk-in clinic. I'd never seen him look this bad.

"Not sick," he said.

"Thought you weren't feeling well?"

"Just sad."

"EmmaDan are fine. Not mad at you. You have an illness Ronny. It isn't really, it isn't your fault."

"Not that."

"What then?"

"Shopping."

"Shopping? Shopping makes you sad? Why? Ronny, you're gonna have to explain...."

"Reminds me of Marcia."

"Okay. But it won't be long before you see her, when we're home."

"Won't matter."

"Why?"

"Marcia broke up with me. Just before we left. Said that I wouldn't help myself, that I didn't *wanna* change. That I wanted her to be like *me*. A drunk. An asshole, like Emma said. She was right."

I didn't know what to say. Said, "I'm sorry, Ronny." Kept one eye on the line of mountains, ghosts on the horizon. And though we drove from one end of the city to the other, they were still there.

"WELCOME TO THE WILD WILD WEST," DAN SAID AS WE ALL stood between the pillars in the entrance to their house. It was exactly what he'd said when we arrived the first time.

Emma had her arm inside his arm. But she let go and smiled and sort of cooed when Ronny handed her the box of salmon and the cedar plank, tied with a blue ribbon. Ronny's idea. Once Ronny handed over the gift, he collapsed. Just like in the movies, in slow motion. Corner of a pillar caught his forehead, opened it up. Emma went stormy, yelled, "For God's sake here we go again, call 911," shoved the salmon box and plank hard into Dan, ran into the kitchen. We both crouched down, Dan sliding his hand under Ronny's bloody head, me lifting Ronny's hand to check his pulse. It was then I saw the black line runnin' up his right arm, from his bandaged hand to just past his elbow. Guess Emma needs some serious schooling in first aid. Before the ambulance came, Mindy showed up and tried to curl up on Ronny's chest, but Emma lifted her away and locked her in the basement.

NEED SOMETHING EASY. TWO JACK LAKE IS THE TICKET, THE guidebook says it's a winding trail, with only a gradual rise till it turns steep then drops off to the lake. Of course, easy is relative. Even at the beginning, I find myself gasping. Doesn't help that it's so hot, EmmaDan says it's been a hot summer here. The peaks of the mountains, usually snowy, aren't. I've been hearing, too, that the glaciers are melting, but can't say I care. Though right now I wish another Ice Age on the whole province.

I come to the rise described in the guide, and there's a big view of Mount Rundle, its serrated face reflected in the lake. I've never been able to see so high, so far, this world about valleys, lakes, towering rock faces—it's shoutin' largeness. Wish it would just shut up. Maybe this is too much nature, too much distance, all this geography standing right up and threatenin' me, like some toothy dinosaur that won't go extinct.

I stagger on. Notice a guy near the trail, crouched in a clearing. He's holding a jar upside down, some kind of flowery urn, is dumping its contents. I assume he's spreading someone's ashes. I wonder what Ronny wants. I know he doesn't want to be buried near Mom and Dad. I wonder if we'll ignore his request. I've always assumed he'll be the first of us to go. I wonder if this thought is a wish in disguise.

Soon, I'm by the lake. Collapse beside a tree stump, but jump up again when I see, on the grain, ants swarming and seething, like beer from a shook can. Then, can't believe my eyes, a big moose cow and her calf break from the cover of trees, splash into the lake. Followed by two figures that, silvery, arrow-shaped, plunge in too. Wolves. They're after the calf.

I drop back, watch from behind a tree, can't break away though I'm also under threat, less equipped than any animal.

The momma turns and kicks, tries to keep her calf between the posts of her legs. The wolves pause. One circles behind. The cow spins just as three more wolves arrive. Momma turns and attacks, drops, sideswipes the smallest wolf, lifts her front hooves. For a moment she abandons her calf. Instantly, a wolf clamps down on the baby's face. Momma rears up, drops, crushes the wolf, crushes her baby. Others race in, yank the calf away. Momma rises, the wolves retreat, charge in again—the smallest falling back, maybe wounded—while the mother appears to forget her calf, pauses and licks the film of blood on her own flank. Attacks again. But it's too late, straight hopeless, it's fucking *done.* The wolves drag the cryin' baby onto the sand, dig in with claws and teeth, while momma moves off, head lolling side to side, into deeper darker water.

I CUT MY MOUNTAIN VISIT SHORT. PHONE RONNY FROM Banff. He'll be in the hospital for one or two more days, isn't sure. The doctor said he was lucky he came in when he did, that he shouldn't have ignored the signs, cat bites are serious business. He's welcome to stay another night with Emma and

Dan, and they're happy to drive him out here on Sunday so he can have his mountain thing, his wilderness experience. I decide no. Decide it's a bad idea. That I should've stayed with him and Emma and Dan. That we can do stuff around Calgary. That we need to spend time in the malls and subdivisions. That we need to fix things there, right there, where our family lives.

THE BOOK ABOUT THE BEAR

NO TELLING WHAT YOU'LL FIND STICKING YOUR ARM UP inside a dead animal. Usually it's stuff you'd expect, junk that morons routinely dump from their cars or SUVs or campers on the side of the road. As if the world isn't already choking on the weird useless refuse of criminal humanity, you feel around for and find, with snapping rubber fingers: cigarette butts and candy wrappers and potato chip bags and coffin-shaped fast food Styrofoam containers, or paper coffee cups with the rims rolled up, or plastic cup lids or, on occasion, a soiled coffee filter. Sometimes, it's an item of clothing: a scarf, a sock, shoelace, baseball cap, shredded leather glove, or the thing that really sets me off, gets my goat—I found one clogging the beautiful throat of a dead wolverine—a disposable diaper.

Also had my share of surprises: once, in the stomach of a road-killed elk, a small Spider-Man action figure. Half a Michael Crichton paperback, *Jurassic Park,* in the belly of a flea-bitten coyote. Long beeswax candle in the digestive tract of a lynx. Perhaps the strangest thing I've found, though, was a perfectly intact Banff snow globe (a good one, glass not plastic, wintry scene of mountains complete with tiny bear and miniature version of the Banff Springs Hotel), in the stomach of a young grizzly that, with its mother, had been struck and killed by a train just outside of Golden, British Columbia.

I've made a collection of the items I've found, at least the unusual things—a still-ticking pocket watch, a baby's rattle—my own ready-made museum, or sad lost and found.

Sometimes, among the omnivorous smorgasbord inside a bear, are human remains, but this is rarely a surprise. Usually, when a bear turns up on the table in my lab, it's because it's torn apart and half-devoured some poor dumb bastard hiker or camper or jogger or unfortunate soul who just happened to be returning at dusk from the Canmore Safeway with some birthday candles he forgot to pick up that morning for his young daughter's party (though his ex-wife had probably reminded him in a series of clipped cellphone texts), and stepped between the momma bear and her cubs. My job is to recover human remains, to determine if the bear that the park wardens destroyed near the victim's half-buried body is the same bear that removed the guy's face, and to send the remains to the coroner. Usually, too, the park wardens give me a report, briefing me on the circumstances of the event, where they shot the bear and how many times, and some data on the victim, if they've determined the identity of the unlucky individual.

This morning, the first item on the agenda is such a killer bear. Mauled some guy in the parking lot at Moraine Lake, dragged his body into the woods. Corporal Troy Esmond, with the RCMP, emailed me a detailed description. The park wardens easily found the bear, followed the button-and-blood trail on the asphalt from the guy's pickup truck to just inside the trees. Also, when the park wardens and RCMP arrived to locate and dispatch the killer bear, a crowd of tourists had gathered in the parking lot and were helplessly watching, at a very unsafe distance, the grizzly swinging its head over its kill. How perverse, and how dumb, can people get?

Sometimes people ask me how I got in this line of work. I love dead things. Knew it in high school. I was one of the only ones who looked forward to the frog and cat dissection. The other kids pegged me right away as weird, not because I was fascinated with guts and things—we all watched slasher films, we all laughed and shrieked when someone had his stomach cut, and guts exploded towards the camera—but because whenever I was working on an animal, I didn't want anybody else to see. Just like my friend, Joey Toehill, didn't want anyone watching him in art class when he painted. I even asked Mr. Wood, our biology teacher, if I could work somewhere else, and he let me use the narrow windowless room where the equipment was stored. I didn't really know, at the time, why being watched upset me. I thought it was because it messed with my concentration. Now I think it was the early inkling of something more profound, that I felt it was wrong for some poor animal to be split open, spread-eagled and pinned in such a public way, to be ogled and winced at by a bunch of pimply kids. Maybe I felt, too, some kinship with the pinned dead animal, as I spent most of my time in school pitched forward, eyes to the ground, avoiding contact with my peers, my badger head pushed back into my shoulders. And I liked the predictability of the animal's insides, not like the labyrinth of the halls, where you never knew what was really there, or who might be creeping up behind you.

I remember thinking, even then, while prodding the thumbprint heart of a cat, or laying the forceps against the raisin stomach of a frog—where, in the body, does loneliness live? Where is *sadness* located: lungs are for breathing, the heart pumps blood, but where does sadness reside? I imagine that animals must feel, at moments, a more pressing, elemental sadness than humans. If nature is "red in tooth and claw," how much more intense and painful might an animal's fear be? Of course, I could never articulate these feelings, at the time. At least, I couldn't share them. The other kids thought I was weird enough.

People still think I'm odd. Going on thirty-seven, I live alone. My friends rib me that I can't get a woman because I'd rather be searching through the entrails of an animal, as if looking for portents, reading the future in the Gordian knot of glistening intestines, and that women can smell it on me. Death perspiration, formaldehyde cologne. No, I know the truth. I'm no Johnny Depp. My face is too thin, my eyes too close together, and my nose is too big, like a snout. My hair's a short but unruly shag, the texture of shredded wheat. And my body is long, lanky, so that when I'm standing facing you, you have to throw your head back, as if you're in a dentist's chair. I tend to hunch over, to offset this effect. My friends tell me I'm cute, that I have an *interesting* face; but beware of that word. And *cute* doesn't make it either, especially when women find out what I do for a living. It's as if, in my profession, I'm the conduit to a graveyard, and I remind people about the dire nature of nature. I'm not the noble veterinarian whose occupation is restoring mended pets to their loving owners. No. I'm the tunnel the animals pass through on their way to oblivion, to flames, and the wild animals I open up will have no marker to commemorate their passing. I do have some women friends, though Bridget, bless her thorny heart, treats me like a charity case, brings me to parties where everyone is younger, and hangs from the loopy rope of my arm and introduces me by my profession. She tells people, usually in a drunken whisper, that I work for the animal version of *CSI*.

Before scrubbing down for the procedure, I make my usual stop in front of the bulletin board near the lockers, study the magazine pictures of animals I've pinned there. I believe that looking at pictures of living animals is an important part of the necropsy process, that thinking about the vital, living creature, remembering that it wasn't always roadkill, confers some dignity upon it. The board is filled with photos of animals looking their best—elk, moose, wolf, coyote, mountain lion, lynx, fox—every creature that might pass through this place. I concentrate on the bear pictures: there's a remarkable profile shot of two bears, backlit by sun, sitting on a muddy bank by a braided river, staring out at something in the water, each with an almost wistful expression. And another of a Khutzeymateen grizzly in a moment of bliss, scratching its back on a bent birch tree, one paw raised as if it's ready to give a high-five.

This morning, the bear is large, a male. It's sprawled bathtub belly up on the hydraulic table, its head dropped back, the black pincushion pads of its paws exposed, claws the cages for small birds. I'm always amazed how streamlined, how well groomed a bear can be, as if it's just strolled from some salon, had its fur combed and coiffed, fussed over. However, I see right away that this is indeed the killer bear, shreds of cloth around the base of its claws, like fabric rings. Each one is spotted with dried blood.

Some fabric, too, in the teeth of the bear. The animal gives me a good grimace as I slide my fingers under its lips, my rubber fingers sticking briefly along its gums. I position the head a little to the side, skull the size of a small child. Even with the animal dead in front of me, the finality of death adding weight to it, I feel diminished, standing here in my rubber gloves, trimmed fingernails, with my assortment of blades and long elbows and prim apron and paper mask. I feel petty and officious, like some purse-lipped bureaucrat.

I move away from the bear. Return with the trolley that holds the tray in which I'll collect the bloody pieces of cloth. I wonder at the circumstances of this particular kill, what the dead man might have done to piss the bear off. Nine times out of ten, a bear attack is the human's fault. A person has blundered too near a fresh kill, maybe the carcass of a deer, and the bear is just defending its food source. Or the person is speed-bump stupid, has taken his pepperoni sticks inside his Walmart sleeping bag, or has left the safety of his SUV to try and get tight with a passing bear (I should start posting, along with my animal portraits, the fatal selfies people have taken in these mountains) believing his camera or phone emits a force field the animal won't be able to penetrate. In any case, the bear is rarely to blame for an attack. Its reactions are logical, consistent, just like the way its insides are set *just so*, as admirable and efficient and beautifully utilitarian as the inside of a Swiss clock.

People, on the other hand, are unpredictable. They often do things that are not in their own best interest. They're blurry in their intentions, and blurry in how they enter your life, then leave it. I suddenly remember how, around a year ago, I wrote a series of animal poems, most of them about bears. But the memory comes with injury attached, with scar tissue: I'd gone home and written the poems after my third date with a pretty woman I'd met through Lavalife, the online dating service. I'd thought our dates had gone well, all of them ending with late-into-the-night conversation at a pub in Calgary, all of them involving a kind of shared astonishment at how comfortable we were together. We discussed the films of Mike Leigh, we were both fans of the music of Tom Waits, and we traded some of our funny horrific experiences of the dating scene, entering into, I thought, a kind of comradeship and warm familiarity in acknowledging how *this* experience was so much superior, so bracing; but at the end of which, on that last night, she announced without irony that she was glad she'd met someone nice, as this was going to be her final date for a while, as she'd decided that, while I was great, I wasn't right for her. When I inquired as to why, she said that she wished she knew, but that something was a bit off, that, even in her enjoyment of our time together, she felt a peculiar distance, an emptiness, like a hollow at the back of her throat. And she told me she was moving to Vancouver in a few months anyway.

Her precise description drew me to her even more, and I felt—even as we stood shaking hands, and she was saying she was privileged to have met me, and as I was coolly deciding that I disliked her eyes, they were a wintry mint colour, and the left one, I'm sure of it, was bigger than the right—a frank hopelessness that mirrored her rush of sincerity. (She *did* seem genuine when she said she had enjoyed my company.) After she'd walked away, I thought of my job. I saw a deer neatly sliced open and steaming on the stainless steel table and felt comfort in this, that I could apply my skills and proceed with assurance to determine exactly why this deer had met its end, what had erased it from the landscape.

Anyway, the poems. I wrote them in a sort of fury. I only remember the first one, but they were all these, I don't know, noble-animal-meets-ignoble-human poems. It went something like:

The bear arrives like a logging truck on the lost highway.
The book about the bear tells how its grille and bumper
will turn you into roadkill.
On its blind way, the book will flatten you
like a rug made from your skin.
You'll find the bear's fur in your kitchen and bathroom sink.

The bear refuses to sleep in the guest room.
In the story of the bear, it will lie on you to tell you a bedtime story.
The book about the bear is a fable without a punchline.
It's a book of gestures, a long-distance call
from a phone booth in the wilds.
The book about the bear is a wish from within that comes true
in a bear attack.
The book about the bear is your story turned inside out.

You're on the table and the bear is dressed in a white lab coat.
It's polishing its instruments and knows
where to make the incision—
from neck to abdomen.
In the book about the bear, it pulls out
your prized organs—the intestines,
the lungs and the heart.
The book about the bear is a coroner's report about
your body and what you do with it.
It's a collection of criminal stories
that depict your life in the wilderness.
The book about the bear has Goldilocks living in Vancouver,
sitting in a café with an ocean view.
You're in the book and so is she and so is the bear.

I wrote, longhand, about five poems in one sitting, my little book about the bear, but I'm no poet. They came out in a rush, and I didn't like the feeling. But I keep a copy close to me, in the lab. I'd like to give it to somebody to read. Sometimes I look at the poems, but can't read them all the way through. They're like the occasional strange thing I pull from inside an animal, out of place and wanting a good scrubbing, funny but wrong too.

I RETREAT FOR A MOMENT, GO TO THE COUNTER AND SINK to retrieve the tools, before I open the bear. I'm well aware of the strange and terrible irony. The precise way I'll be entering the bear is nothing like how the victim entered. And, although one might blame the bear or the specific victim in this case, I can't help feeling that, in the end, we're *all* to blame—we've infringed upon the territory of bear, its primordial and private landscape, so the bear must take, in a token of rebellion, the occasional sacrificial victim. I salute the bear in this. And I shall hold my knife up in celebration of the lost cause that the bear keeps undertaking, how it keeps rummaging through humanity, person after person, darkness after darkness, until it comes out the other side.

I return to the sprawled creature and begin to raise the blade, when I hear a faint chirping sound. I assume that a sparrow, outside, is singing close to an air vent, or has somehow found its way inside the building. With the fifth and sixth chirps, the sound muffled but distinct, I know it's no bird, and my eyes fall to the great body in front of me.

And I think, *this is new, this is clever*. And remember how I knew this day was going to be, well, strange. Earlier, on the way to work in my pickup, I had to brake and evade, in the middle of the road, a white-tailed deer, like a lightning-struck living ornament bearing down to fasten onto my hood. Weird thing was, the big buck had only one antler, protruding from the side of its head like an open hand, so the animal appeared off-centre, off-kilter and afflicted. After the close call, I shuddered and hugged the steering wheel, trying to pull the whole truck close, and sensed it was going to be an off-kilter day. That feeling swells up again when I hear the sound and understand what it is.

A cellphone. A cellphone ringing, inside the bear.

I don't move right away. Put my head to the bear's abdomen. Can feel the vibration. It is as if the bear has come back to life, for a moment, with a kind of hunger that won't quit, won't let death get in the way. I take the twelve-inch knife, make a bold incision. Open the abdominal cavity to get at the stomach, where the object is located. I let myself rest on the edge of the table, feel a sense of comfort, my arm right up inside the bear, the cellphone hard against my fingertips. It's an invasive thing, a malignant lump, and, soon, anger starts to rise in me. The phone is so, well, unnecessary, symptom of a disease of the modern world. I work it loose, I'm hurrying things, won't mention this in my report. Something milky coats the object, and something like string, a cellphone pouch made of fabric and viscera and blood. I free the phone, it's like tearing open a little change purse, then place it to the side of the tray. A small flip phone. Get a disinfectant cloth from near the sink and wipe it clean, see that the metal is a kind of rust colour. Maybe bear juice has already corroded it. It makes another noise, a trilling, four-note sound.

Someone has left a message. I wonder who might be calling. Surely the family and friends of the dead man have been notified. The mauling happened yesterday. Perhaps it's some telemarketer, selling bear spray or a subscription to *Strange Wilderness Tales*, ha-ha. Or it's a remote acquaintance of the victim, someone not close enough to warrant being told about his demise. Or perhaps the flip phone doesn't belong to the unfortunate man. Perhaps the bear swallowed it earlier, lapped it up along a trail, although the location of the phone inside the bear's stomach, entwined with remnants of the victim, tells me the bear swallowed it in the attack. I'm relieved I hadn't recovered the phone in time to answer it. What would I have told the person on the other end? I'll return it to the RCMP, maybe it will shed some light, or perhaps the victim's family will have some use for it, although I'm not sure they'll want it, under the circumstances. Of course, the RCMP can tell the family they found the phone near the victim's body, no need to share the grotesque details. Although I conclude that they *should* be told—the man's technology didn't protect him from nature, didn't help, maybe even contributed to his death. And I imagine, too, that a flip phone might be desirable to an animal, that something so old school might be consistent with what I imagine is a wild creature's more basic tastes.

The phone begins to ring again.

I take off my paper mask. The buzz is inside me. It is like the shouting, the whining of the dying man. Stupid bastard, what are you doing inside the bear? Can't you leave the animal, killed for your sake, well enough alone? I pick up the phone, flip it open, have to wipe some juice away, press it to my head. I regret that I removed my mask, as if some contamination might lick its way inside my brain.

"Yes?"

"Jesus, Ethan, I left four messages. Why didn't you answer? Are you okay?"

It's a woman's voice. I have the impression, I don't know why, that she's someone from the victim's workplace.

"Ethan, are you there? *Ethan*? I can't stand it when you go silent on me."

"This isn't Ethan."

"Oh. Is this the wrong number? Is this 433-8173?"

"It's the right number. I think."

The woman goes silent. At first, I think we've lost the connection. When she speaks again, there's a difference in her voice, a brusque, businesslike edge that has replaced the urgent familiarity.

"So who is this? Is Ethan there?"

"No. But you probably have the right number. I'm not sure, because I found the phone. It's not my phone. I found it."

I decide that I'll tell the truth about Ethan's phone once the caller has identified herself. That is, if she isn't family, isn't someone close to the victim, though she seems to be. How will I determine her exact relationship with the deceased?

"Found the phone? Where? Where did you find it?"

My tongue is large in my mouth. It's tired and doesn't want to budge. It's hibernating. I think of telling her to contact the RCMP. But that would be a giveaway, a hint about the tragedy. Perhaps I'll keep the phone, shut it off and store it among my collection of artifacts, place it between the orthopedic shoe insert and the hearing aid.

"In the forest. I found it in the forest. To whom am I speaking?"

"I'm a friend. The *owner's* friend. You found it in the forest? Where, exactly?"

She's a friend. That could mean anything. But there is suspicion in her voice. Maybe she thinks I'm a thief, that I stole the phone. I resent her tone. I'm tempted to give her the shocking news, *Hey, I didn't steal it, I just now fished it from inside the stomach of a bear, I'm afraid the phone was just the appetizer before the bear feasted on the entrée.*

"On a trail. Near Moraine Lake. In Banff. This morning."

"Oh."

I can hear her breathing. Her breathing is loud. I imagine her lips close to the phone, they're thin and severe and painted with two slashes of red, and for a moment I can smell her lipstick, it defeats the cold scent of the metal.

"Do you work with Ethan? Maybe you could return the phone to him."

"No. You can keep it. Don't think I'll be seeing him again."

There's an absence in her voice. It occurs to me that maybe she's playing some perverse game. Maybe she knows what happened but she's letting the reality settle in slowly. Maybe she's still digesting the hard facts and feigning ignorance, phoning his number and hoping against hope he'll answer, that the terrible news she received was a case of mistaken identity or a bad dream. *Don't think I'll be seeing him again.*

I think about giving my condolences, still not sure what's happening. Never sure with human beings. I want to get back to the bear. Want to grip the handle of the knife, to wield it. To return to what I know. This thing in my hand is awkward, too small to get a grip on, and the reception is imperfect. There is a crackling noise that coats the woman's voice, sets it on fire.

"Why do you say, I don't understand, you won't be seeing him again?" If she already knows, it won't hurt to ask.

"Where did you find it, exactly? In the grass or in the open? Did it look like he dropped it?"

"Yes. In the open."

"On a trail? Near Moraine Lake? In the open?"

"Yes. On a trail, in the open."

"And you were hiking there? By yourself?"

"Yes, by myself. Why?"

"Never mind. Keep the phone. Caveat Emptor."

"What?"

"Nothing."

"I can bring you the phone. You can give it back to Ethan. It's no trouble. Are you in Calgary? I could meet you."

"Thought you found the phone near Moraine Lake?"

"Ah, yes, but no. I'm in town now, in Banff."

"Can't believe he lost it. Jesus."

"People lose cellphones all the time."

I can hear her snuffling back tears. Or maybe it's static. Then, "Oh, it doesn't fucking matter. Sorry to bother you."

"Wait."

Surely the family knows by now, someone, mother or father, perhaps wife, would have had to have gone to identify Ethan's remains, would have had to endure that unendurable moment. Friends informed. This person isn't in close contact with his family, but she's obviously more than an acquaintance.

"Maybe he'd like it back," I try. "Does he have a land line? I could phone him. Or you could tell me where he lives."

"Believe you me, he won't want that phone."

"But who are you?"

I'm out of my league. Playing at being human. I'm a bear come out of a long, cold sleep, ice packed into the corner of its eyes. My brain's a glacier. I'm the bear on the table, revived, but with humanity in its stomach, stuck in its throat.

"Look, I'm a friend. What's it to you? The phone was a gift. He lost it. Or threw it away."

I try to imagine what sort of woman buys a man a flip phone or what kind of man might want one. I dismiss the thought, picture the guy now, his body beneath the bear, face enlarged by terror, stretched the size of the bear's head, and the bear whispering in his ear.

"Maybe he didn't. Maybe he had an accident. Maybe he didn't just throw it away."

Then she says what shuts me up, what shuts me down, sews me closed: "I don't think his *wife* will want that phone."

I can hear her breathing, again, on the other end. End of the line. I look at the bear on the table.

She says, with a blade in her voice, "What do you mean, accident? Do you know something? You sure you just *found* the phone?"

I put the phone down. Shed my rubber gloves, drop them on the floor, untie and drop my apron. Go lean against the hydraulic table, against the bear. Fur rasps along my sleeve. Lift the phone again. Feel a stitch in my side, a quick stabbing pain, as if someone has poked me hard in the ribs.

"Yes, I found it. But there's more to it. I mean, I know a bit more." I can't believe I'm opening myself up to this. But it's too late to close the phone. Too late to replace it and bury it back inside the bear. To go back to earlier in the day, into the warmth of my bed or the coffee and wire smell of my truck. I've entered something different. I know more than I want to, but don't feel empowered, am embarrassed by what this woman, in her sadness, has revealed. Feel as if I owe something. Her voice implicates me—her voice, and its history of disappointment. I have a debt to pay. I also realize that, although she doesn't fathom it yet, I'm her only connection to what happened, and to Ethan. She won't hang up on me.

"What the fuck? What do you know? Who are you?"

I'm improvising. I need to make things right. I started this. I could have ignored the phone. She would have found out anyway, there will be a news report in the paper, on the radio and Internet, maybe already is. I try to picture her, again, imagine what she looks like. Can't. Can't concentrate. I picture something crumbling, like that desiccated thing that arrived in the lab last fall, an old cougar that died in the crevasse of a glacier, then was spit out and spent weeks baking in the sun. Collapsed into dust when I opened it up. I imagine this woman collapsing into dust. I see myself carrying her, trying to contain her. Concentrate on what I am going to say. On making the present lie seem, well, less of a lie. I tell myself I'm protecting her.

"Look. I found the phone. But I know something about Ethan. I mean, just by chance. Can't tell you on the phone. At least, it would be better if I could tell you in person. I know that he didn't just throw the phone away. We can meet in a coffee shop. I don't mind meeting you. I'll tell you what I know. Today, if you like. This afternoon, if you like. You can trust me. We'll meet in a public place, if you're worried...."

She doesn't respond. She won't be meeting Ethan this day. I'm a poor substitute. And the news will be, well, bad. Very bad. I have the sense, maybe I'm wrong, I have the sense that she needs to hear it from a person. I've been close to Ethan, for better or worse. I opened up the cave of the bear, last resting place of her friend. Lover. Don't know what I'm getting into. But I feel as if I'm liberating Ethan from the bear. And I'm liberating the bear, too, from that encounter. I'll have to figure out what to say. I'll have to be ready for her collapse. How will I? I can say I found the phone, but that I also happen to know what became of him. Or should I tell her the truth about how I found the phone, about what I do? Perhaps, in the time before we meet, she'll get the news about his death. That'll make things easier. Or worse, if she doesn't understand why I lied. But if she hasn't heard? This is no dissection, no necropsy. I don't know what's inside this woman. Don't know what I'll find. Not a plastic toy, or a snow globe. No telling what you'll find when you enter, like a probing hand, into another person's life, sudden as a bear attack. What can I offer? How will I play a part in her grieving, a grieving that, presumably, will be constrained by circumstance? Don't know how to proceed. I'm scared. I hope that she says no, that she gives into her anger and cuts me off. Sweat is beading in the palms of my hands—I can hardly grasp the phone. It's suddenly as slippery as it was when I first plucked it from inside the bear.

I decide I'll show her something. I'll show her my book about the bear. Maybe that will help. I feel as if the bear, somehow, must make amends. And I'll tell her my story, and all the stories I've collected, over the years—my little museum of stories. I'll try to explain.

Then she says, quietly, so that I have to close my eyes to hear, "Okay. My name's Connie. What's your name? I'll meet you halfway, if you're in Banff. Can you meet in Canmore? At the Communitea Café, on 6th Avenue, at 3:00? Are you free, then?"

DISCUSSION QUESTIONS

1) The story "What is Written" is narrated by a paroled convict. Which of the other characters does he most connect with, and why?

2) In what ways does the landscape reflect the relationship between the two sisters in "Athabasca"?

3) Describe the central conflict of "Attacking the Bear."

4) In "Rudy," what is the protagonist trying to accomplish? Why does he believe it so important to connect with the couple on the trail?

5) Why does the narrator of "Three Places" finally "modify" his wife's wishes?

6) How does the style of "Marilyn in the Mountains" contrast with the other stories? Why do you think the author uses this approach?

7) "From Castle Mountain" dramatizes a little known chapter of Canadian history—why do you think this history is not better known?

8) In "Goth Girls of Banff," what are the reasons that Linda quits the self-styled profession of Goth Girl, while her sister continues?

9) In "Natural Selection," the character of Ronny is associated with images of evolution, as in the title of the story. Why does the author include these details?

10) Why does the narrator of "The Book About the Bear" answer the phone? Are his actions appropriate or questionable?

11) What are some of the elements that unify the stories in this collection, aside from the location?

ACKNOWLEDGEMENTS

Earlier versions of some of these stories appeared in *Prairie Fire*, *EVENT*, and *The Antigonish Review*. My thanks to the editors of these magazines, with grateful remembrance of the late Andris Taskans of *Prairie Fire*.

"What Is Written" won second prize in the 2014 Sheldon Currie Fiction Contest—a shout-out to Sheree Fitch for choosing it—and "The Book About The Bear" won a Manitoba Magazine Award for Best Story. The manuscript as a whole was one of three finalists for the 2014 HarperCollins/UBC Prize for Best New Fiction.

Thanks to Matt Bowes, Claire Kelly, Isabel Wang, Christine Kohler, and everyone at NeWest Press for their help and guidance, and to Kate Hargreaves for her excellent cover design.

Big thanks to Anne Nothof for her precise and thoughtful editing.

Thanks to Lee Gowan, Patrick Crean and David Bryan for their helpful suggestions, and to Dr. Ian Barker of the University of Guelph for sharing his knowledge of necropsies.

Thanks to Andrea Holzinger for sharing her knowledge of migraines.

Thanks to Jason Pichonsky for the video.

Thanks to Clive Holden for his help with the website.

Thanks to the Ontario Arts Council for awarding me a Works-in-Progress grant.

Thanks to the Banff Centre for the two writing residencies.

Long overdue thanks to the staff of Senator O'Connor College School, especially the outstanding English and Arts Departments—Patricia, Christine, Priscilla, Ian, Juliet, Catherine, Kat, Samantha, Anna, Lorraine, Lisa, Nicole, Leanne, Vera, Julie, and Josie, Nancy, Irene, Patrick, Val, Stuart, Amy. Also, Emma and Luisa. I was blessed to work for all those years with such a talented and selfless group of teachers.

Thanks for the blessing that was the life of Tom O'Brien.

Thanks to Paul and Doug and Betty for that first trip to the mountains.

Thanks to Tony Labriola for his help with earlier versions of the manuscript, and for his ongoing passion and friendship. I will never forget.

The story "From Castle Mountain" is respectfully dedicated to Dmytro and Katarina Chaban.

The story "Natural Selection" is respectfully dedicated to my late brother Jimmy.

JOHN O'NEILL is the author of the novel *Fatal Light Awareness* and four poetry collections, *Animal Walk, Love in Alaska, The Photographer of Wolves,* and *Criminal Mountains.* He was raised in Scarborough, Ontario, where his parents worked for many years as building superintendents, an aspect of his history explored in *The Photographer of Wolves.* He was a winner in the Prairie Fire Long Poem Contest and Sheldon Currie Fiction Prize, and the recipient of a "Maggie"—a Manitoba Magazine Award—for Best Story for his "The Book About The Bear." John was a finalist, with his manuscript *Goth Girls of Banff,* for the HarperCollins/UBC Prize for Best New Fiction. He taught high-school English and Dramatic Arts for twenty-nine years, and now lives and writes in the Leslieville neighbourhood of Toronto. He and his artist wife Ann make frequent trips to Canada's Rocky Mountains, and this landscape continues to be a major influence on his writing.